D1087080

ALSO BY KURT A. MEYER

Noblesville

THE SALVAGE MAN

THE SALVAGE MAN

BY KURT A. MEYER

Little Rock, Arkansas
2015

This is a work of fiction. All characters, organizations and events portrayed in this
novel are either products of the author's imagination or are used fictitiously.

THE SALVAGE MAN Copyright © 2015
by Kurt A. Meyer ALL RIGHTS RESERVED

Edited by Joe Formichella

Cover design by Gable White

www.RiversEdgeMedia.com
Published by River's Edge Media, LLC
100 Morgan Keegan Drive, Ste. 305
Little Rock, AR 72202

Manufactured in the United States of America.

Softback ISBN-13: 978-1-940595-24-5

Ebook ISBN-13: 978-1-940595-25-2

For my son, Cal, who came along on many
salvage excursions and as a child lived
out the meaning of this story through the
relentless force of a willful, open heart.

CHAPTER 1

Dan drove out the long straight stretch of Main, past the courthouse square, the bank drive-thrus and tire shop parking lots, then the Victorian homes and their multicolored front porches, and finally past the '50s and '60s era ranches until he reached what was once considered the edge of town.

It was a warm, dry day. Sunlight shone bright in bleached splatters across the asphalt beneath trees that crowded the road. His black hair, slashed with slender ribbons of gray was tousled by the breeze from the open window.

From the dashboard speakers pulsed the staccato hammer of power chords strung together by a looping lead guitar. The cell phone rested in the console cup holder, plugged to a cigarette lighter adapter that fed his Spotify alt-county playlist to the truck radio. Wilco's cranking guitars settled into an easy rhythm. His hand rocked on the steering wheel, the outstretched thumb tapping to the beat. At random points the bass overtook a blown door speaker, distorting the song with ragged, breathy jolts.

"Outta site, outta mind, indeed," Dan grumbled to the scene beyond his dirty windshield.

This place felt more like countryside in his youth, on a bicycle on a day not unlike this one. Amid the old houses with huge yards that sat sprinkled along the mile of countryside for over a century, little prefab ranches, Levittown like boxes built by National Homes had cropped up just before and after Dan's birth. Since then, slowly, a trailer park grew, partially hidden behind a big old house on a slope to the river. Now newer houses clad in drab vinyl colors, grouped on clean, monotonous well-tended culs-de-sac, gobbled up entire fields. Instead of seeming expansive and solid, as it had in his youth, the street felt claustrophobic and temporary, just like his own life. Because the street transformed in small pieces over forty years, he'd gotten used to it as it was. Still, on a day like today his mind wandered back to his boyhood and he remembered the fields that once dotted the landscape.

Dan clearly recalled the soft hissing of a breeze coming across the tassels of corn, looking like a yellow wave on an ocean, rising and falling gently. Dogs, some friendly, some mean, would dart off the big porches and run alongside his bike. He'd stop to pet one or pedal like hell to get away from another, his head tucked low between the handlebars, straining against the wind.

When he got lost in such memories he was momentarily taken off guard by the town's changes, feeling he'd taken a wrong turn and landed in a foreign town, not his town. And the surrounding countryside was like that no matter which direction you drove. This all felt personal. *How is your life any different?* was a question his train of thought usually found its way to when he started cursing growth and how it had turned his town into a near-foreign landscape.

"Hell, your *own* life is a stranger," he mumbled, adjusting the rearview mirror. These angry, embittering thoughts had come to consume his inner voice over the past decade. He'd seen a poster on the wall in the local coffee shop with a quote attributed to Buddha, "What you think, you become." He was just barely introspective enough, sensing at the edge of awareness that this is how once proud, hopeful young men become grumpy, angry old men—curmudgeons. A montage of mental video clips rolled through his mind when he wasn't on task; his ex-wife, his old job at the piston works, the house where he grew up, his life after the kids went off to college, and every argument, failure, insult, or dark moment he'd ever had in life, they increasingly just ran in a constant loop in him mind. Hell, sometimes he unwillingly found himself imagining disputes and confrontations that hadn't even happened.

"What you think, you become." It was happening to him. He was doing it to himself. And he sensed it, but couldn't stop.

He steered the truck with his right hand and rested his left arm along the open window. The sleeve of his thick, white, cotton T-shirt fluttered in the breeze across his tanned, tight bicep.

A black BMW rushed toward him in the rearview mirror and passed quickly on a double yellow, like he was standing still. Dan grunted and shook his head, "Racing to a red light. The whole fuckin' world is racing to a red light." His truck lumbered up behind the BMW and stopped. When the light turned green the black car shot forward, darting left, out of turn, ahead of oncoming traffic.

Dan sighed heavily, proceeding on his way, to yet one more thing he didn't really want to do. He neared the right-hand curve where the river begins to converge with the road beyond a line of trees. There, a shallow, wedge-shaped, two-hundred-acre expanse to the west, perhaps the last bit of land in cultivation between this side of the river and town, came into view. "Bein' in the flood plain will keep you safe from developers a bit longer," Dan mumbled to the land and the corn.

As he eased into the big, gently banked turn to the east, the gable end of the Ballard farmhouse came into view above the trees. The gaping windows hung dark and empty. The deep eaves cast harsh shadows along the length of the house. Tangled branches of long neglected trees surrounded the red brick house and seemed to tether it to the ground. He slowed and swung into the driveway.

On both sides of the gravel drive, grass left uncut for a couple years rose up two feet. Here and there renegade maple and poplar trees sprouted. Beyond the entrance to the drive, yellowed grass was matted down to dirt by tire tracks. Between the garage and the barn, perhaps three hundred yards away, Dan could see yellow, earthmoving equipment grinding away at fields that grew corn just last year. A few trucks and cars, the vehicles of the heavy equipment operators, were parked about. Dan parked and got out.

His truck had been impressive once, eight years ago when he bought it new—four wheel drive with an extended cab, bed liner, CD player, two-tone paint job, the works. But now the tires were nearly bald, the snap-down vinyl bed cover had ripped to shreds and been discarded, and there was a whale of a dent in the driver-side door. Dan had stared down a loud-mouth punk in Syd's Bar a couple years ago, thinking he'd scared the kid out of starting a fight, but when he went out to his truck and found the big dent with a dusty boot print at its center, he realized what the kid had meant by, "You'll be sorry, old man."

He scanned the side of the old brick farmhouse. This place was familiar. Though he'd never been in the house or any of the out buildings, as a kid he'd played in the woods that lay thick to the east of the barn. There, the trees crowded a ravine running down to a stream that spilled into the river some hundred yards to the north. He and his friends had made forts among fallen trees by the stream and played army.

He turned back to the house. There were large brackets, or 'corbels' as the antique dealers called them, nestled in the eaves. They would bring some money. There was a simple side porch with turned posts that were worth a little and a front porch with a bit of gingerbread that someone had kept well painted. He could get several hundred bucks for the stuff on the outside alone. The side door wasn't worth taking but the front door had heavy appliqué trim that arched to frame two glass panels. He would take it.

Women considered Dan a handsome man. Not like a model or athlete, but like a man of hard work and purpose; lithe, yet muscular, tanned, weathered, and more fit than most men half his age. He didn't work out. He worked. He walked about the buildings, examining the barn, garage, and grain bin, moving in purposeful, determined strides as if he intended to do something important when he got there. His female contemporaries often whispered to one another, "It ain't fair that a man his age can look so damn good."

From behind him a gleaming black Hummer lurched around the side of the barn, bending the tall grass down before entering the matted parking area. It stopped right beside

Dan's truck. A short man in a sport coat and jeans, cowboy boots, and a waistline that spilled over his belt hopped out and walked toward Dan.

"Hey, Tom, how ya doin'?" Dan asked. He wedged his hands in his pockets, trading glances between his shabby truck and the Hummer.

Tom strode up confidently and stuck out his hand. Dan fumbled to pull his hand from his pocket and took Tom's palm awkwardly, noting how unnecessarily firm Tom's grip was.

Tom smiled a big toothy, Teddy Roosevelt grin from behind a pair of sunglasses and a thin black mustache. "Know what I was thinkin' 'bout as I came around that barn, knowin' that I was meetin' you here? I was thinkin' of all the times we used to ride our bikes out here when we were kids and played down there in the woods. Boy, the Japs and the Germans didn't stand a chance against us," he laughed.

Dan smiled and looked down at the ground.

"Boy, that was a long time ago," Tom squinted.

"Another life ago," Dan put in.

"Ain't that right." Tom rocked back and forth on his heels in a moment of awkward silence.

"Well, what do you think of her?" Tom finally asked, leading the way toward the house. "Think there's anything here worth a dollar?"

"Don't know. We'll have to take a look inside."

Tom produced a handful of keys and they went in.

They wandered the rooms of the house, their footsteps echoing off old plank floors and falling silent on aging green shag carpet. The downstairs was empty but for a few random items left behind by the last tenant.

Dan was not prone to mysticism. Still, he got feelings about the houses he stripped. Some of them reached out to him like a warm caress and he'd feel guilty for stripping them, knowing they'd be torn down soon. Others filled him with a sense of dread as he came through the door. "Something bad happened here," he once found himself mumbling. He worked at salvage that day with a tingling at his spine, adrenaline goosing him as he worked. He'd drive away from those chilling places avoiding eye contact with the darkened windows, afraid he'd find a ghostly face glaring out at him and shaking a fist.

But this place was hard to peg. As they moved from room to room the vibe of this once graceful, now tattered house veered from welcome to foreboding. Bright rooms with their ceilings reaching skyward, and tall, hopeful windows drawing in sunlight promised that fresh paint and refinished floors was all this place needed. But in the darkened shadows of stairwells, rank bathrooms, and the tiny twentieth-century closets cobbled into the corners of nineteenth-century rooms, a coldness overtook Dan and left him feeling hollow and unwelcome and wanting nothing more than to tell Tom he wasn't interested and leave.

But he couldn't leave. He needed the job.

Dan stopped to run his hand along an elegant, turned walnut newel post. The rest of the woodwork was unpainted and made of an assortment of hardwoods. He knew he could get money for the artificially grained doors, the balustrade, and the spindles, but showed no emotion. Tom tried and failed to make small talk with his old friend as Dan inspected hardware and floor grates with silent care.

The stair landing split in two directions; five steps going up toward the front of the house and its original two bedrooms, and five steps leading in the opposite direction into the 1870s addition.

A shadowed, cavernous, second-story room made up the addition to the back of the house. It was entered by one door to the north, and a back staircase to the kitchen at the south end. There, a disturbing sight stopped them. A foam mattress lay on the floor in one corner, covered with a dirty, unzipped sleeping bag. Beside the mattress sat a water bong with an inch of dirty water at its base. Sixteen-ounce cans of PBR were scattered about. Dan nudged one can with the steel toe of his boot and found it was full. Never opened. "Too stoned to realize they had one more left?" he mused.

"See why I need to get this place leveled?" Tom said. "Kids keep getting in and partying. Something bad's gonna happen if we don't just wash our hands of this place ASAP."

Yellowed wallpaper had released from the walls in full, intact sheets, gathered like ribbons of fallen pasta at the base of one wall. On the exposed bare plaster, the anarchy symbol had been spray painted, its circle reaching from baseboard to ceiling, with long narrow drips of black paint running down the horizontal slash of the letter A at its center. Two spray paint cans lay on the floor amid wads of paper toweling, each with a fat dot of dried spray paint in the middle. Dan kicked a bundle of stiffened paper towel with his foot.

Tom shook his head. "They've been huffing. And smoking weed. And drinking beer. Scares ya, don't it? I worry about running into one of those kids, all jacked up on that shit."

"Smells like a gas station men's room in here." Dan shook his head and walked toward the back staircase. He stopped to shake his head yet again at the sight of a used condom on the floor. "Jeeezus. It's a sad ol' world," he mumbled.

Back outside, he walked around the house, noticing that shutter hooks were still in place on every window; something he seldom saw.

"Is this stuff worth anything?" Tom asked. Dan thought Tom was digging to settle on a price for salvage rights. He offered his usual story.

"Well, it's worth money, but not to most people. Ya see, if it was all sitting here on the ground with the nails pulled and the hardware separated and all cleaned and everything, then you'd really have something. But to get to that point you have to do some hard work, have to get dirty and spend days on ladders and loading and hauling. Once you figure in your hours spent getting it to where you could sell it, well then it ain't worth so much ... in its current state ... if you see what I mean."

Tom was impatient. "The labor it takes to salvage it accounts for much of its value," he said.

"Yeah," Dan agreed quickly, "that's a good way to put it."

"Do you want the stuff?"

"Well sure, Tom, but we've got to agree on a price first."

"No price," Tom said. "Just take it. It's yours. If you don't take it, it'll go to the dump."

"Well, thanks, Tom," Dan smiled, now freely offering his hand to shake on the deal. The mood was suddenly relaxed.

"Saw Sue the other day eatin' popcorn shrimp at Applebee's," Tom said, changing the subject. "She waved and said howdy."

Dan's upbeat mood evaporated. He looked at the ground and shook his head. "We've been divorced three years now and still everybody tells me what's goin' on in her life." He looked away and bit the back of his lip. "You'd think we'd gone for a walk and lost each other in the woods or somethin'."

"I'm sorry," Tom said, shaking his head. "I think of you—I think of her."

Dan shook his head, too, and smiled insincerely, waving

off the apology, mumbling, "Aw, hell, how are you s'posed to know how I feel about it when I don't even know?"

Tom pulled a phone from his pocket to check the time, then shot quick glances beyond the barn through the narrow opening of trees to the earthmoving equipment working in the distance. "I got another appointment. Gotta run."

"Well, thanks again, Tom."

"Hey, I'm just glad I could help you," Tom said with a broad smile, slapping Dan on the back. He got in the Hummer and shot across the grass, toward the workmen and the clouds of dust their machines were raising to the south.

As the car disappeared, Dan mulled over those words, *'glad I could help you.'*

He saw now that Tom had never intended to conduct a business transaction. He meant to do charity, to give him a handout. Even if Tom was trying to do him a favor, it wasn't any less embarrassing for people to know he needed one.

Could it have been Sue? Was she the one who asked Tom to help me? Aw, hell, he thought to himself, *who cares.*

Dan looked back at the house, the two-car garage, the little brick shed behind the house, a board and batten shed between the garage and the barn, and then the barn itself. He could make some money from this old stuff all right, but he needed money now—today. Rent was due tomorrow. He had that money, but he needed some groceries, too, and didn't have enough for both. He had to find something he could pick up and take now. Something that wouldn't take a lot of time to remove and clean up.

He looked in the little brick shed behind the house. Originally a milk house, it had only a few old paint cans on the floor. He peered into the garage. Garbage was scattered around. Nothing of value. He didn't even bother with the shed next to the garage, but went on to the barn instead.

Straining with the full weight of his body, the sixteen-foot-tall door, lashed together by metal supports in a Z, gave way. It dragged on the ground but he got it open enough to wedge himself through. It was musty and dark inside. He found a metal post on the ground and gouged it into the dirt several times, digging a long seam beneath the door. Finally, he managed to open it fully. Light streamed into the massive space, casting long shadows beyond trash and old lumber. He picked about in the pile of wood, old planks, and fence posts. Buried among the debris he found three, turned, matching, Victorian-era porch posts, all in decent condition. He quickly pulled them out and dropped them in the thick grass outside.

He climbed the ladder to the hayloft. A few birds scattered overhead, lighting on the hulking, hand-hewn beams above him. He had been in these dank places before and they always made him uneasy. Underfoot were planks that were low-grade lumber when new. A hundred to a hundred and fifty years later they were rotted, some were missing, and many he couldn't see because of the hay and straw scattered about.

There was a stack of some sort in the corner to his left. Doors perhaps? He scanned the light coming up between the cracks of the planks, looking for the beams below so he could step on firm structure. He flipped open his cell phone for a bit of light and walked closer.

He hated these places, these barns with nesting birds and rats and mice and reptiles, with the smells of old rotting manure and hay and earth saturated with decades-old gasoline and oil and livestock urine. He stepped forward, keeping close to the shadowed line of a beam below. Nearing the stacks the shapes became clear in the cell phone light. Shutters.

Kneeling before two neat stacks of shutters, he strained to lift one up for examination, but it wouldn't move. A finger run along the length of each stack revealed both were bound with bailing wire. Reflexively he reached for the leather tool pouch looped to his belt, unsnapped its cover, and pulled out the all-in-one tool. He'd used the plier-shaped tool so many times, lack of light was no impediment. With automatic precision the bailing wire was wedged into the crotch of the pliers and cut easily.

The shutters were old, probably made well over a hundred years ago. The good ones were stacked gently before him, the bad ones he tossed carelessly aside. They shattered on the loft floor with a loud crash, sending dust rising.

They must have been put there long ago, for exterior shutters had a short life. The wood joints and moving parts did not fare well in driving rain, summer humidity, and winter snow and ice. Dan figured they had likely spent more years sheltered in the barn than they'd spent on the house, because most were intact. A few had broken louvers and all had badly peeling, dark green paint. Bird droppings covered everything he touched. He just wanted to get the good ones out and head to Indy. Another with tattered louvers was tossed in the waste pile and splintered, sounding like a tree branch wrenching loose in a storm.

Suddenly, something moved near Dan. He caught a glimpse of it in his peripheral vision—an arm and a head coming at him. He stood in one jerking motion and swung around to face it. His right foot plunged through a rotted floorboard and down he went.

His ass hit the loft floor and he slammed into the planks, flat on his back, one leg dangling below. He shot defensive glances about with his arms raised to protect his face.

Nothing. Echoing silence.

Dan looked about the loft. It was as big as a small basketball gym. But there was no one there, just him, alone.

"You fool," he mumbled aloud. "You nervous and jerky fool." He momentarily searched the rafters for whatever it was that had scared him, perhaps a pigeon or squirrel. Nothing.

Back to his feet, he brushed off his jeans.

An hour and a half later he was leaving the antique salvage shop with two hundred and fifty bucks in his pocket, cruising north on Delaware, eager as always to leave Indianapolis behind him. His hands on the steering wheel were still dirty, his hair peppered with cobwebs.

As he swung onto Fall Creek, making his way toward the interstate, Junior Brown's black-tar, retro-country baritone crooned from the dashboard speakers, a steel guitar crying for lost love.

CHAPTER 2

Sue had never set foot inside Dan's place, the shabby little world he moved to when their neatly ordered lives together unraveled for good. She made a point of not being home when he moved out and later made an even more particular point of not driving within a block of his new place. Couple weeks after he moved out, in the middle of a sleepless night, overcome with regret and longing, Sue slipped on some jeans, a sweatshirt, and flip flops and walked the eight blocks from her place to his along the lonely streets, knowing she wouldn't wake him and not sure what she really meant to do. She was just heartsick and wanted to understand.

Standing just out of range of the alley intersection streetlight, she took in the sadness of the once grand home, now split into four rental units and encased in chalky-white aluminum siding and black plastic shutters. Weeds grew up along the foundation and Dan's truck was parked in a gravel drive along the side of the house. It looked to her like a tomb. Why would he choose that rat-trap, alone, rather than a life alive with her?

Sue's chin quivered, and a tear trickled down her face. She walked back home no wiser. From then on she avoided both streets to the north or south, or at least avoided looking toward that house, much as she averted her eyes away from the cemetery when she drove down Monument Street, so there was no chance of seeing her mother's grave.

That night Sue had actually conjured a pretty accurate picture of Dan's sorry little place in her imagination. His was one of four tiny apartments in what had once been a single-family residence. Someone chopped it up after World War II. His living room was originally a side parlor, his bathroom a former enclosed side porch, his kitchen was half the original kitchen and the bedroom was half the original dining room. It was a virtual paneling/dropped ceiling showroom. Over the years all repairs were done as quickly and cheaply as possible—and it showed.

Home from the day's salvage, he opened a beer and a bag of chips and plopped down in a chair that once sat in the basement rec room in the house he and Sue had raised the kids in eight blocks away. It was still odd to him that he had worked so hard for so long to make a nice place to live and now he was here in this dingy little place and Sue had the house. She had the nice furniture, too.

He'd wanted it that way. When she asked for the divorce, he wasn't really surprised, but he was wounded and wanted her to feel guilty. Still, on the surface, in the place where he was able to think and feel about it, he blamed himself. So he'd insisted, quite foolishly, that she keep the house and whatever furniture she wanted. His lawyer was stupefied and insisted that Dan not tell anyone who'd represented him.

Once, during negotiations, with Dan and his attorney on one side of the table and Sue and hers on the other, she even reached across the gleaming oak table, topped with a half-inch-thick piece of glass and gently caressed Dan's hand, saying in a hushed, desperate whisper, "Dan, please! Surely you want something more for yourself."

"It's only things," he said. "Things are easy to get."

It was his way, to be generous so that it made her feel petty for taking it. But she hardly knew what else to do. Give it to Goodwill and let them both live with nothing? Not Sue. If he wanted to be a fool, fine, his choice. But not her.

After the divorce, after he moved out, he continued to come back and do odd jobs for her. She never asked him for help, which was fine because his pride wouldn't let him do it if she'd asked. He'd let himself into the garage and get the mower or a snow shovel and take care of what needed doing—but only on the outside. After the divorce, he seldom went inside. If she was home when he came over, Sue came out and talked to him. Small talk mostly. He came inside only twice each year. Once on Thanksgiving, when Sue had the kids and both families over for the day, and again on Christmas, when they sat around the tree in stiff chairs and awkwardly exchanged gifts. The other eleven months he treated the house like a graveyard, a place where he didn't really want to go, but when he did, he went with reverence for things passed-on.

There was never hostility between them, just a melancholy sort of distance, a sadness for things left unsaid. Sue would sit on the front step and smoke a cigarette, watching him rake the yard and wish she could bridge the distance that had grown between them over the years.

She never wanted to divorce him, but the distance was so painful, the wall between them so tall, and she was so anxious to get on with life in some meaningful way that she threatened to file for divorce, thinking it would shake him out of his shell—his cocoon—his personal tomb.

As the kids progressed through high school, as the Japanese bought the piston works and became his antagonistic employer, as she worked longer and longer hours at the bank, Dan seemed to recede into an inner space, some inner world. The young, affectionate, spontaneous teenager she'd fallen in love with thirty years earlier had grown into a silent, cold man. The threat of divorce didn't change him, and when it was time to sign the papers, there didn't seem to be a good reason not to.

But still he came to mow the lawn or shovel the walk for her. She took it as a sign of remorse—Dan's tiny, inadequate, olive branch. Or habit.

"He's sorry alright," Sue once said to their daughter, Kristin, "but don't blink or you'll miss it. He's got his emotions wedged down so deep inside it'd take a stick of dynamite to shake 'em loose."

Still, she came out and sat on the steps and made small talk with him out of some faint hope that he might utter the words that would put their lives back together again. He never did, and she didn't really think he could, but Sue was bound by commitment, she couldn't make herself stop trying. But her trying got more and more half-hearted as the distance between the divorce and the here-and-now dragged on.

Dan sensed bits and pieces of these realities in his own numb sort of way. Sitting there in his little apartment, sipping a beer and eating potato chips for dinner, there was a faint recognition that this was his place now, away from Sue, but also disbelief that it had actually happened.

In the distance, the earthmovers crisscrossed the old cornfield in seemingly aimless swaths, slicing up roiling seams of soil and dragging them, slowly tilting their blades until the dirt fell away in low spots. They were making unnaturally perfect hills and valleys, trying to make what God had seen fit to create the northern two-thirds of Indiana without: contours.

Dan picked through the piles of lumber in the barn and carried an armload of likely candidates to the front yard. It was a lovely, clear, dry summer day. Beneath the canopy of hackberry and maple trees that partially shielded the house from the ever-busier road, he worked on dismantling the front porch. He used a hacksaw to cut the nails that held the upper gingerbread skirting to the porch posts.

The scissor jack from his truck was placed alongside one of the posts. An eight-foot-long, rotted four-by-four was forced between the jack and the decorative porch skirting. With a few turns of the jack, the porch roof lifted with moans and creaks, just half an inch, just enough to pull the posts free. One at a time, Dan pulled the posts loose of the toe-nailing that held them to the horizontal supports that the roof rafters rested upon. He replaced the turned posts with old lumber from the barn so the roof wouldn't pull loose from the house and collapse.

The weather and the setting were lovely and peaceful. On the road out front it seemed for a short time that the town's relentless, manic, whining and humming and thumping traffic eased. The work felt like a joy, like a really wonderful thing to be allowed to do. Dan stopped from time to time to lean against an enormous maple and watched the yellow earthmovers. He knew it was just a matter of time—months at the earliest, a couple years at the most, before this place would become what the rest of the town had become—foreign. But this morning, this spot still felt like the country, the way these places felt when he was a boy.

Just then, as Dan was feeling so good about the moment, his eyes strayed to the big, blank, six-over-six windows dotting the brick facade beneath and above the porch and he thought of the mattress on the second floor and the people ... kids maybe, who had used the place to party. He imagined them huffing paint, or their mouths inhaling deeply against the bong, water bubbling and smoke spiraling up, or two stoners having sex on the mattress. His initially positive sense about the house changed. A shiver rose up his spine. Suddenly he felt menace, as he had for that moment in the barn when he mistakenly thought something lunged at him.

Tom hadn't left him with a key and Dan forgot to ask for one, so he pulled back the door to the cellar and stepped down into the darkness.

The cellar, with its fieldstone foundation, was pitch black and damp. He felt his way along the walls, his hands running across the cold shapes of the stones, his arms like feather dusters gathering cobwebs. The interior steps became apparent and he made his way up the narrow flight and found a doorknob.

Dan stepped out into the musty hallway between the dining room and the kitchen. He opened the front and back doors and propped them open with stray bricks from the yard. As he looked back into the front room with its twelve-foot ceilings, he felt something, and at this moment it wasn't fear at all—more like expectation. He needed to stop worrying about homeless junkies and get to work.

When all the posts were stacked in the truck, he spent the rest of the morning prying the gingerbread skirting free.

A salvage man can go about his work with a careless freedom. The common house builder or remodeling man has to worry about scarring the paint on the clapboards or denting the vinyl or aluminum siding. Not a salvage man. Dan cranked up the extension ladder and carelessly let it fall hard against the white trim band that held the big, ornate brackets supporting the eaves at the top of the second story. As he wiggled the ladder into place amid the overgrown grass, loosened paint chips fluttered down from above and nested in his hair.

Dan climbed up and pried around the top and back of one of the big brackets. They were massive. Each was made of seven separate pieces of wood. The pieces on either end presented a deep relief, beautifully cut in delicate scrolls. Three of the inner layers of wood were cut slightly smaller than those between which they were sandwiched, adding to the visual feast these pieces of woodwork brought to the house. Whoever kept the porch detail well painted all those years did right by the eve brackets too. These were worth big bucks at an antique salvage yard.

As he pried the first bracket loose, exposing the shanks of the square nails that held it into place, he considered the odd nature of chaos and order as he so often did when tearing an old house apart.

As a boy he had once sat in his filthy bedroom and pondered the nature of the mess. The mess had been so easy to make. Cleaning it up, as he had been ordered by his mother to do, would take a while. Even though it might take him an hour to clean it well, he knew he could then run through it with his arms spread wide, knocking things from shelves, tearing the sheets from the bed, and completely undo the hour of hard work with fifteen or twenty seconds of reckless abandon.

He had asked his science teacher, "Why is it so hard to clean up a mess, yet so easy to make it?"

Mr. Mills had grunted dismissively without looking up at him, "The universe is constantly moving toward a state of disorder—chaos—entropy."

That answer had never satisfied Dan, but he had been a wise enough boy to recognize that maybe his dissatisfaction with the answer had come not so much from doubting it, but from wishing it weren't true.

He worked at the bracket, gently prying around the perimeter on both sides until it pulled free. It couldn't be dropped from up there without breaking the brittle poplar wood. He climbed down, set it gently in the grass, nudged the ladder over a bit, and climbed back up.

From where he worked his body was directly in front of the second story windows. He could look down and into the bedrooms that had faced the road since years before Abe Lincoln took office. This second bracket was held tightly in place. He'd been able to begin loosening the first one simply by wedging his pry bar into the cracks between it and the band board. This one needed more persuasion.

Dan pulled a framing hammer from his leather tool belt and beat at the elbow of the pry bar, wedging the bracket out, opening a quarter-inch seam in the paint between it and the eaves overhead. He positioned the bar between the bracket and the band board and began hammering it again to wedge it free on the backside. The metallic clank rang in his ears.

Suddenly, he was startled by the shout of a shrill human voice. The words were lost among the concussive clang of the hammer. He stopped and looked about the yard. No one. Then, Dan jumped and nearly lost his balance when he saw a woman standing no more than two feet away from him on the other side of the glass in the upstairs bedroom. There was rage in her face and again she yelled, "What are you doing to my house?"

In the few seconds he stared, shocked, into her eyes, her expression evaporated. The pinched muscles of narrowed eyes and gritted teeth fell loose into embarrassment and then opened wide into shock, not at Dan, but at her own outburst. She put her hand to her open mouth with a start and stepped backward, dissolving out of view amid the reflective glare of sunlight and clouds in the glass.

Dan clung to the ladder that he only now realized was swaying beneath his feet, having been struck hard by the startled, stiffening jerk of his legs. His heart beat wildly against a metal rung. He climbed down quickly and stepped backward through the deep grass, looking up at the windows, searching for another sign of the woman.

Someone living in the house ... he wondered to himself, *a homeless druggie, squatting in this place?*

Breathless with anticipation, he waited for her to reappear. She did not.

Dan stepped around the east side of the house, splitting glances between the upper windows and the excavators across the field. He hoped to catch a glimpse of Tom's black Hummer, wave him over, and figure this thing out. Tom was nowhere in sight.

Finally, Dan went to the side door and called out, "Whoever you are, I don't mean you no harm. I've got permission to be here and salvage things."

No reply.

He walked back around front and looked up at the windows again. No sign of the woman. He poked his head in the front door and shouted, "Hello. You in here, lady?"

Again, nothing.

He knelt down in the doorway and looked up the stairwell. From there he had a full view of the central hall and up the stairs to the landing. No signs of life there or in the front room.

Dan gingerly stepped inside and called out again. "My name's Dan Reynolds. I live here in town. I've got salvage rights to this house. I don't mean you no harm, but the Woodview Acres Corporation owns this house. They gave me permission to work here."

He continued to speak as he crept gently up the stairs, looking up and over his shoulder through the spindles of the upstairs hall balusters. He knew she could run down the back stairs, in fact hoped she would, hoped she'd tear down those stairs and out the back door. But he heard no sounds other than the echo of his own voice.

"You know, I've got no argument with you and don't really care what you've been doing here," he spoke out loud as he met the landing, his hand sliding along the turn of the bent wood railing. "I've had some hard times, too. Made some mistakes. I know what it's like to have to scratch a bit to get by. But you can't be in here. Woodview's got other plans."

By now Dan was at the top of the stairs, his heartbeat throbbing in his ears. He pulled the hammer from the tool belt and held it ready, just in case she came at him. He shot quick glances into the room where the woman had been and stepped gingerly toward the doorway.

"Like I said," he went on, calling out loudly, but in as friendly a voice as he could muster, "I got no argument with you, but you can't party here." He moved into the empty room and looked about. There was nothing, just the rungs of his ladder outside the window. He went back across the hall to the other bedroom doorway. "If you just go ahead and leave now, nobody needs to know you been living here. I won't call the cops or anything."

That room was empty, too, but he'd only looked in front rooms. He walked slowly toward another doorway to the back two-thirds of the upstairs. He peeked into the next room, which again, was empty. There was just one room left. The one with the anarchy symbol on the wall.

As he moved toward the doorway he spoke again with a firm, friendly voice, "You know, I'd feel a whole lot better about this if you'd answer me. I'm walking along here with a weapon drawn, not sure what you're thinkin' or plannin' to do. Why don't you just call out and let me know where you are?"

There was still no answer. He was now in the open doorway to the huge back room. He stepped in and looked around. No sign of anyone. His eyes followed the slit between door and door jamb, looking for anyone hiding behind it. Nothing. He stepped farther into the room and walked to the back staircase.

Where did she go? He'd heard no movement besides his own.

Then behind him, at the front of the house, he heard a soft creak, perhaps someone on the front stairs. He moved back toward the door.

Just as he crossed the threshold, a voice from behind startled him nearly out of his skin.

"Why are you tearin' up this house?" she asked in a soft, yet insistent voice.

Dan spun around. There she stood, the woman he'd seen through the window. She hadn't been there before, he felt sure of it. There was nowhere to hide, no closet or alcove, only the back stairs and the door he'd come through. He'd seen and heard nothing just a moment before, yet there she was. Then a thought, *Maybe she'd been laying on the mattress.* The mere thought of the bizarre circumstances made him shudder.

She stood at the far side of the room near the back stairs, bolt upright posture, hands folded together in front of her. They were far apart, so he couldn't see her well in the dim light. Her blonde hair was pulled back tight behind her head. Her long dress skimmed the floor.

As he spoke, his hoarse voice betrayed the tension of the moment. "I'm sorry if I scared or upset you, but I've got permission from the Woodview people to do salvage on this house. They told me nobody lived here. And whatever you've been doing here, you gotta stop and get out."

"Why are you taking things off the house?" she asked.

"These things I'm taking off have value on the antique market. If I don't take them, they'll be lost forever."

"Why lost forever?"

"Woodview is gonna tear this place down, all the outbuildings, the barn ... they're gonna level the whole thing. They've subdivided the land. They're gonna build new houses."

The woman took this in, clearly shaken.

"You can't flop here," Dan said. "There's a Red Cross office in town if you need some food or a place to stay. We don't have any homeless folks around here much. Everybody's got too much money for that, but they'd know how to help you, somehow."

"Well, you do somethin' for me," the woman said, her voice shaking. "You tell Mr. Woodview that he mustn't tear any of this down. There's not a thing wrong with any of it that a fresh coat of paint and a little love won't fix. You tell him."

Awe fuck, Dan thought to himself, *She's nuttier than a fruitcake.*

"Listen," he spoke out loud, "paint and love won't save these buildings from ... progress. Hundred and fifty years ago somebody wasn't smart enough to know that twentieth-first-century sprawl from Indianapolis was gonna bear down on this place, Ma'am." Dan slipped the hammer back in the tool belt. "It can't be stopped."

"Now, I mean it!" she said, stamping her foot on the wood floor, "you tell this Mr. Woodview that it mustn't be done. Now go!" she insisted, waving her hand to shoo him away. "You just go and stop taking things off the house and you tell Mr. Woodview what I said."

Dan knew for sure now she was not mentally right. Either tripping or mentally gone. Or both. He would just leave and call Tom and let him get this gal out.

"Alright," Dan said, "I'll go and tell him what you said. Don't get upset."

He turned and started to go, but halfway through the middle room he turned back. That glance stopped his heart in shock and confusion. In just the few seconds since he'd turned away from her she had silently moved half the distance across that big room, toward him. Her head was cocked to one side to watch him go. But stranger still, her hands were no longer folded, they cradled a bundle—it looked like a baby wrapped in a blanket.

"Now I said for you to go and I meant it!" she said, more firmly than before, like a mother scolding a child.

Dan was unnerved. He shot through the two bedrooms, down the stairs, and out the front door. He frantically pulled the keys from his front pocket and jumped into the truck, fired it up and swung around in the driveway, his cooler tumbling off the tailgate and into the yard. *Forget the road.* He instead made his way for the dusty ruts the excavators had made across the field—had to find Tom and let him straighten this out.

He couldn't stop himself from looking up at the house as his truck lurched across the side yard. A chill ran through him when he caught sight of her—the pale, angry face in the window, glaring out at him.

Dan never found Tom, but left a voice mail on his cell. Later that evening Tom pulled up outside Dan's apartment.

"You say there's some woman living in the house ... with a baby?" Tom asked through the aluminum screen door, examining the tiny, poorly furnished apartment. He noticed an opened, steaming, microwave meal box and a can of beer on the table in front of the TV.

Dan was embarrassed to see Tom standing at the door. He quickly swallowed a mouthful of food. "Yeah, some woman. Was wearing a long dress," he said, getting up from a tattered Lazy Boy. He walked toward the door, wiping his hands on a kitchen towel. "I don't know if she's a Deadhead or a Phish Head, or a meth-head, but let me tell ya, she ain't right. Wanted me to tell you to stop your plans to tear the house down."

"And she had a baby with her?" Tom squinted, incredulous.

"Now I never actually saw a baby," Dan said, jabbing a palm in the air, "but all of a sudden she was holding this bundle ... looked like a baby wrapped in a blanket."

"I called the sheriff's department and they said they'd send somebody to meet me out there at 6:00. That's in about 15 minutes if you wanna follow me out."

"Sure, I'll follow you out there," Dan said. He left his dinner, climbed into his truck, and followed Tom out Main Street to the farm.

Once they'd pulled into the yard, Dan felt a little foolish for leaving all the doors and windows open and his ladder up against the house.

"You didn't close the place back up before you left?" Tom asked, stepping out of his car.

"This woman wasn't right," Dan said, pointing at his head and twirling his index finger. "I didn't want to stay around long enough for her to freak out on me. She was dressed all weird and wouldn't listen to reason."

Tom quickly made his way toward the house, but stopped, rubbed his chin, and walked back to the Hummer. "If that's the case, maybe we oughta just wait until he shows up." Tom opened the back door of his car and pulled a hanger off the seat, took off his sport coat, and hung it from the overhead peg in the back seat.

A sheriff's deputy pulled into the drive and parked in the tall grass. He got out and nodded a "howdy," to Dan and Tom. He looked like an ex-Marine—jarhead haircut and a chest full of muscles so hard and smooth it looked like his perfectly pressed shirt was painted on his body. The deputy adjusted his gun and nightstick and radioed his arrival to a dispatcher.

Dan retold his story as the three men walked around the exterior of the house. They placed several concrete blocks over the cellar door to block that exit, then went in the house through the front door.

"With two staircases and multiple exits, let's lock this behind us so we can sweep the house and know that it's clear as we go," the deputy said, gesturing in abrupt motions with a long black flashlight in his hand. "We're not trying to trap her, we just want to know that the house is empty once we're done. One of you stand here at the bottom of the stairs and watch, another go and stand at the back stairs. I'll sweep the downstairs and then up. I'll bet you've scared her off, but we'll just make sure. If this person has an infant with her this could be a matter for Child Protective Services."

Dan stayed at the front stairs and Tom went to the back. The deputy searched the basement with a flashlight and walked the rooms of the downstairs, peeking in each closet. He met Dan.

"Where was she when you spoke to her?"

"Upstairs. In the big room at the back."

The officer went up and called out "Hello?" as he went. Dan could hear his footsteps echo through the house as he moved toward the rear. Eventually he came down the back steps.

"Nobody here," he proclaimed. "And that little squatter's party pad ... doesn't look recent to me. But, I'm not a forensics expert."

"What do you mean, not recent?" Tom narrowed an eye.

"There was dust on top of the beer cans, and water evaporated from that bong. Could've been six months ago."

They locked the back door and headed for the garage. They checked each outbuilding. The garage was empty. The timber-framed grain building had only one door and that one was secured with an ancient, rusting padlock. The barn, too, was empty. There were no signs of anyone.

Tom stopped in the front yard, sighing toward the house and shaking his head. He turned to Dan. "For liability reasons, this kinda worries me. Do you have a hammer and some nails in your truck, maybe sixteen penny?"

"Yeah."

Tom rolled up the sleeves of his white dress shirt, and nodded to Dan, "Then let's nail the doors and windows shut."

Dan gave Tom a hammer and between them they nailed the back door and every first floor window shut. They gathered some two-by-four scraps from the barn and battened the doors closed on the outbuildings as well. Only the front door of the house was left passable. Tom locked the dead bolt and handed the key to Dan. "Well, that takes care of that," he said. "I don't imagine our visitor will bother you anymore.

"Got a little somethin' done, didn't ya?" Tom said, standing in front of the Hummer in the tall grass, squinting up at the stripped porch.

"Yeah, it's gonna take me a couple-few days to get all those brackets down."

Tom examined the ornate bracket laying in the yard where Dan had left it earlier that day. He reached down and tilted it to the side to inspect the floral pattern. "People can't do that kinda work anymore."

"Oh, they can," Dan replied. "They just don't."

CHAPTER 3

The next morning Dan resumed his work in the eaves. By noon he'd stripped the brackets from the front of the house and stopped to eat a bologna sandwich in the front yard. He sat on the tailgate of his truck, sipped a Coke, and looked up at the second-story windows.

With a double-take shock and snap of the neck, he saw her. She stood in a front upstairs window staring down at him. Their eyes met. She made no move to hide herself. He stood in disbelief, holding the Coke can in his hand, gazing up at her with his heart pounding furiously in his ears.

His disbelief gave way to frustration. "God, fucking, dammit!" he moaned through clenched teeth, scowling down at the grass.

She motioned to him, waving him in, not in a friendly way, but in an insistent way, as if she meant to discuss something of importance. She turned and disappeared.

"Shit!" he shouted, throwing the can into the grass. "I don't have time to be social-fucking-services!" He sat back down on the tailgate and composed himself, considering the situation.

There was no way for her to get in. He went to the front door and checked the lock. He jerked on the knob. The dead bolt held fast. He stamped around the house, checking each window. None were broken. None would open. There was no other way in.

Back at the front door he fumbled with the key, dropping it on the stone threshold. He was not really afraid of her, he was afraid of the circumstances—a homeless woman going to desperate measures to live in this old place—a meth-head with a flop house, whatever. There wasn't anything really threatening about her expression or demeanor. But he didn't want to end up responsible for helping her, and he couldn't leave this job, he needed the money. This needed to be sorted out, now.

He opened the door and stepped into the central hall. "Hello?" he called out sharply. Just like the day before, she did not answer. He headed slowly up the stairway, twisting his neck back to watch the landing and rooms beyond the balustrade above him. It was embarrassing to do it, but again he gently slid the hammer from the tool belt and held it ready at his side.

Then, from some distant corner of the house came an echoing whistle—four simple notes, two quick beats of the same note, with the third longer and rising, then falling on the fourth. It was a calling sort of whistle, the kind a parent might use to get a child's attention from afar or perhaps to call a dog. It unnerved Dan. *She's taunting me.*

Dan reached the top step and moved into the first bedroom. But he knew she wasn't there. For reasons he couldn't have explained if he tried, he knew she was waiting in the big back room, standing alone in the vast, dark emptiness of that space, and he knew she meant him no harm. Intuition was not something he trusted. Still, he was certain enough now to feel foolish for holding the hammer as a weapon as he used it to push the next doorway open, like James Bond stealthily nudging a door open with a gun.

He stepped through the door, into the darker space beyond, and immediately saw her. She was near the little window that looked out over the backyard. She stood, twenty feet away with her back to him, gazing out the window. He slowly stepped a few feet into the room toward her. Over her shoulder and through the window he could see the yellow bulldozers and scoop shovels moving in the distance, one disappearing behind the deep green leaves of a sugar maple that shaded in the backyard.

"Those big yellow machines will be here soon to knock this place down, won't they?" she said, staring, still watching them prowl the old farm fields.

"Yes," Dan replied.

She turned to his face without a word. Even from that distance he could clearly make out her facial features. She was probably in her midthirties. Her blonde hair was pulled tight behind her head in a ball, the crisp hairline framing delicate, pale features. Her arms were crossed. Her expression impassive. She wore a long dress bound tightly around the waist that touched the floor.

In a whisper that sounded like resignation, she asked, "When?"

"Oh, not right away," Dan said, feeling oddly responsible for it. "They won't get back here for a couple weeks, at least. I think they want to get going on Phase One down there first so that builders can start on the models, then they'll turn their attention to this end."

"There's no way to stop it?" she asked, turning back toward the view of neatly contoured building lots and curving roads that were taking shape amid surveyor's stakes tipped with red cloth.

He was prepared to address her with his parental impatience, but Dan stood motionless, listening to the sound of her words float like effervescence through the room. There was a strange, AM radio, treble-tone clarity to her voice, a purity unscarred by use or abuse. Base notes seemed to tune in, then out. He noticed, too, the fluidity of her movement. Though he had only seen her move her body twice now, her neck arcing her face toward and then away from him, there was something pure and inhumanly graceful about her. Like her voice, her movements were astonishingly smooth, otherworldly in an alluring way, unhindered by age or earthly frictions. She didn't seem drunk, or tweaking, or stoned. But something wasn't right with her. He was assembling this data, looking for common threads, trying to make sense of the moment. He looked to the mattress and debris, searching for signs of activity. The cans and bong and bedding appeared untouched.

Facing him again, she made purposeful eye contact. He felt it clearly as a restatement of her question.

"No, I don't think so," he quickly and self-consciously replied, waking from his examination enough to answer. "No way to stop it that I can think of."

She paced the floor toward the side window, her arms laced together across her stomach, cradling her breasts that were bound tightly in a close fitting, snugly buttoned top. He continued to watch her move with interest. Her steps were not normal. They were normal in the sense that they were fluid, purposeful steps, but they were to normal walking what lip syncing is to singing. Her actual footsteps didn't seem to completely interact with the floor as they should. It occurred to him that they, too, were silent. As he shifted his weight from foot to foot, the floor creaked. She walked about the room, but made no sound. Though ill-defined, these impressions fluttered through his mind as she took another look out the east window.

"The barn? The grain bin? The milk house? The carriage shed? They'll knock all them down, too?"

"Yes," Dan answered. "When they get done you won't be able to tell that any of this was ever here."

She turned and walked closer, ignoring for a moment the world she'd been watching beyond the windows, concentrating instead on him. She stopped within six feet of him and ran a nervous hand across her forehead. "It's got nothing to do with you, right? It's those men here with you yesterday, lookin' for me? They're doin' this ain't they?"

"You were here?" he grimaced, puzzled. "You saw us? How could that be? We checked every place."

She dismissively shrugged her shoulders. "Them men, they're the ones doin' this all?"

"Only the short man in the Hummer, the one with the mustache. He's part owner of the development company that's putting in this addition ... Ballard Woods."

"Ballard Woods?" she asked, her eyebrows raised with interest. "Is that what they're namin' this little town they're makin'?"

Dan nodded his head, still carefully examining her facial features, the translucent nature of her skin, the almost glowing aura that hovered about her.

She endured the examination. "That's my name," she said, studying him back, less with wonder and more with purpose, watching for his reaction. "Ellen Ballard."

Dan continued to scrutinize her face, lost in the growing realization that something was not right about this woman. "You can't f-flop here," he stuttered, nodding toward the mattress. "Whatever you're doing here, I don't care, but you can't stay."

A sly, dismissive smile spread across her lips. "That's not mine. I scared them kids away weeks ago. They won't be back."

He narrowed an eye at her.

She breathed softly, "What did you do with the shutters you took from the barn? Did you hurt yourself when you fell through the floor?"

Then, without warning, she was in front of the back window again. She moved from one place to the other like an overlapping fade-out, fade-in in a movie. In a fraction of a second she moved to a space twenty feet away. Her back was to Dan. She spoke as if not terribly concerned with him.

"Go ahead and run off if ya want," she said. "Everybody else does."

"How did you do that?" Dan asked, his voice trembling.

"Don't be afraid to believe whatcha already believe. You think you know, but you're afraid to believe it, so ya ask me, hoping I'll tell ya something that explains it, something that will explain away the ember that's already catchin' fire in yer head, the one that scares you."

"Are you real?" Dan asked. "Is this really happening?"

She turned and looked at him with an almost caring smile. "Oh, I'm sorry, I misunderstood. Yer not doubting me so much as yer doubting yourself. Are you afraid you're crazy?"

Dan nodded his head.

"Oh, I'm real enough," she said warmly. "And I ain't seen anything of you so far that says yer crazy. Go on to yer second thought."

He watched her from across the room. In another second she faded out of her spot by the window and reappeared directly in front of him, her expression unmoved.

"Yes," she said quickly, "I s'pect I am. Does that frighten you?" she asked softly, tilting her head to one side.

He took in her words, slack jaw, without reply.

"Please don't be." There was a faint hint of pleading in her tone. "I can't hurt ya, and wouldn't even if I could."

A chill rolled like an ice cube sliding up his back, conjuring a shudder. His jaw trembled. They stood facing one another in silence for a few moments. Slowly her expression gave way to sympathy for him and his confusion. She saw the hammer at his side fluttering gently in his trembling hand.

"Sit down, Dan," she ordered firmly.

He hesitated. "How do you know my name?"

"That's what Tom—the man with the mustache," she drew a finger across her upper lip, "that's what he called you yesterday when you two were nailin' things shut. Now sit down ... right there on the floor ... you really do need to sit down."

He half-sat, half-collapsed with one leg sprawled straight out and his arm rested on the bent knee of the other. She faded out and then back in, in front of the window, her back to him once more.

"I have gotten good at acceptance ... in my current state. I know I can't stop this thing from happenin', as I've been unable to stop anything in this physical world. I suppose I understand what yer doin' and why yer doin' it. I have no quarrel with you and wish ya no harm. Though it hurts me to see it happen, I guess I don't mind if you take things apart. At least somebody will have use of some of these house parts. That's what yer doin', right?"

"Salvage," Dan replied.

"Yes, salvage. I understand. Go ahead with yer work and I won't bother you no more." She turned to look at him over her shoulder. "I gather you need to work. I'll let you do your work."

"You were in the barn?" he asked. "Were you the thing that startled me?"

"The thing?" She giggled. "Yes, I'm sorry. I really had it in my head to scare you away, but I lost my nerve at the last minute. Didn't have the heart," she said playfully.

He really wanted to leave the room, to get away from her, away from this moment, so he stood. "I guess I'll just get back to work," he said cautiously.

"Yes," she said, turning away, "best get back to work."

Dan made his way hurriedly through the upstairs rooms and down the staircase.

One of Dan's most significant childhood memories was of diving too deep in the reservoir. He plunged so deep his ears hurt. With that painful warning he arched his back up and looked to the surface only to realize the great distance he had to close before breathing again. He struggled toward the surface in a panic he'd never known before. With each frantic arm stroke he became more desperate until finally, mercifully, he broke the surface of the water, heaving deep gulps of fresh air.

His journey from the cavernous back room and the ghost named Ellen was much the same. He moved without running, but wanting to set each purposeful step into a leap, feeling he was being watched, being examined the entire way. He crossed the threshold as if he just leapt from deep waters, sighing with relief.

Back in the yard Dan paced across the trampled grass in front of his truck, trying to make sense of it all, taking a few deep breaths and reminding himself that he was a mature adult, not a child afraid of the dark after a scary movie. He was determined to stay and keep working, figuring that was the best way to keep his wits. He walked out to the road and watched the corn sway in the sunshine, trying to concentrate on something as mundane as the blades moving slowly with the breeze, clearing his mind.

By the time he trudged back to the house he felt numb, his mind frozen between the need to continue working and the encounter with Ellen.

He moved the extension ladder around to the west side, climbed up, and began working at the first bracket, as if in a trance, his mind far removed from the work. He got the first one down and started on the next, only to see her—Ellen —standing by the window watching him work. He tried to ignore her, but it proved impossible. He felt nauseous and sweat gathered thick on his face. He didn't want to stay, but needed to. Climbing down the ladder, he sat in the grass for a moment and closed his eyes, leaning back against the bottom rungs, taking deep breaths.

For years Dan had felt increasingly divided, apart from the world around him, seeing himself more and more as an outsider in his own hometown, isolated from his family, his wife, and his children. And now this—this incredible event. It could not be shared for anyone would surely think he was crazy. He prayed several times to wake up, but the birds in the trees around him continued to sing and Ellen continued to watch him from the room within the big brick house.

When he reached the fourth bracket, above a window farther down the west side, she moved along with him, and watched.

She called through the window, "Ya know the house didn't have them brackets on it when it was built in '48 ... 1848. When my husband was older, in 'bout '68, his second wife pestered him to add on the back section and change the style a little. Used to be the house was just the front part that faces the road, but they added the back part, doubled the size, built it in this Italian style, added the porch and the brackets to the front as well so it would all match."

Dan didn't reply to any of this, but nodded and smiled as best he could. He went on to the fifth and then sixth bracket. She changed windows again. Eventually it was just too much for him.

"Well, I've gotta go," he said to her, slipping the pry bar and hammer back into his tool belt. She smiled and nodded from behind the pane of glass, her face framed by the wooden mullions.

He gathered his tools and ladder and the brackets that were scattered in the grass and loaded them all in his truck. He felt her eyes upon him, whether they were or not, and climbed into the truck self-consciously. As he pulled out of the driveway, he looked up at the house and saw her standing in a front window, watching him leave. That cube of ice ran up his back again and the hair on his neck stood on end. She waved at him as he turned onto the road. He waved back halfheartedly, feeling foolish for doing it.

Moving down Main, into town proper, he wanted desperately to do something normal, something that would make him feel normal. He drove over a few blocks and down 16th Street, passed their little house—Sue's little house. The lawn needed mowing. He pulled into the drive and got out, went around to the back door of the garage and let himself in. He lifted the overhead door, filled the mower with gas, and pulled the starter.

Dan mowed the yard as he had hundreds of times for more than twenty years. Although today he tried to force the image of Ellen Ballard from his mind, as fascinating as it was. *Useless*, he thought.

When finished he brushed off the mower with a broom and swept the sidewalk and drive. The short toot of a car horn woke him from his working trance. He looked up to see Sue behind the wheel of her new car, pulling into the drive. She waved at him and he stepped aside, into the grass, giving her room to pull into the garage, then resumed his work.

Sue eased out of the car, well-dressed and carrying a briefcase, a cigarette wedged between two fingers on her free hand. She stood for a moment at the edge of the driveway, watching Dan sweep.

Sue had aged well. She had very nearly kept her general figure, neither gaining nor losing much weight. She worked hard with makeup to hide the well-defined wrinkles earned from years of sunbathing and cigarette smoking. She colored her hair to hide the gray. In the sun it looked a slightly unnatural brownish red, a color no one is born with. It didn't look bad, but it did look colored.

"As always, thanks, Dan."

He forced a smile, "Old habits die hard."

"You okay?" she asked. "You look ... bothered about something."

"Oh ... maybe the heat's just gettin' to me."

She sat on a step and rested her briefcase against her leg. "Got a call today from the reunion committee. They're wondering why they haven't heard from you and thought maybe I knew whether or not you were planning to come to the reunion."

"Reunion?"

"Duuhh. We graduated thirty years ago, ya know," Sue smiled. "Sometimes it's hard to believe it's been that long and other times it seems like a century ago.

"Well, what do you say; are you going?"

Dan mulled it over. He shook his head slowly. "I don't know how I feel about it, Sue. I mean, sometimes I wonder what I have in common with those people. It'd just feel weird. I don't belong there."

"This is your hometown, Dan," Sue said, gently incredulous. "This is where you belong. If you don't belong here, where do you belong?"

"Dunno," he grunted.

She watched him sweep the final blades of grass into the street. "Well, I'd like to stay out here and talk to you but I got plans tonight," she said, not really wanting to hurt his feelings, but still, wanting him to be reminded that she was seeing someone. "Need to change my clothes, ya know."

He shook his head in understanding.

"Kristin called me today at work, said she was coming home tomorrow night. The first summer session is done. She'd like to spend some time with you."

"She knows where to find me," Dan replied, finishing up.

Sue could feel it in his tone, the way he tried to make her feel sorry for him ... or guilty. Stupid thing was, the present state of affairs was his fault. And they both knew it. *Typical man.*

She disappeared into the house. Dan couldn't deny that it bothered him that Sue was dating someone. It made him burn inside. It was a late-fifty-something widower who lived in a big house on the lake and drove a big car and did important things at the bank. A man transferred in from some corporate office when the bank was bought out. Add to that the fact that Kristin coming "home" meant that she was coming home to a place that was not his home—not anymore.

He went home to his little apartment, his home, and opened a beer, drank it half down, sat the can on the edge of the bathroom sink, and took a shower. When he was done he stood in front of the mirror looking at his reflection. He felt better now, like maybe this thing that happened in the old house had been a dream. Looking deeper still into his own face, he studied the wrinkles, wondering how he'd gotten here, to this place, this moment, this age, to this phase in life.

It was his generation that had really cranked up the youthful view of the world, making grown-ups, except those too old or too smart to care, feel a bit out of place because they weren't young. He half considered things he'd carried from his youth and nurtured, kept alive, long beyond the time when he should have let them pass. And here he was now, looking in the mirror and not knowing how to take this face that stared back at him.

He thought, *Our culture prepares one for and celebrates being sixteen—twenty one—twenty five. There are few honestly glamorous role models for being fifty. Instead we're shown actors and actresses who have worked out for hours a day and been pulled, sucked, tucked, waxed, hair-plugged and rebuilt by cosmetic surgery, trying to look thirty-five again so that they can smile on the cover of a grocery store checkout aisle magazine for an article titled, "Fit at Fifty," as if the way they looked was normal, or even a mature, rational goal for someone nearly half a century old.*

Where are the real role models for being fifty? Dan wondered.

CHAPTER 4

Dan couldn't afford it but didn't feel like cooking, so he drove to McDonald's and ordered in the drive-thru. He parked in the lot and ate in his truck, remembering the old barn that in his youth stood right where McDonald's was now. He'd played in that barn as a child. Ted Floyd, who lived on the farm, once on the edge of town, had been his friend. He and Ted and Tom would arrange the bales of hay in the loft to make tunnels and hideouts and played cops and robbers and cowboys and Indians in that mammoth space with its wooden skeleton visible above.

Ted was long gone. Selling all this land for the building of schools and fast food restaurants had made the Floyds rich. Ted lived in southern California now, was a bearded, fifty-year-old, mediocre artist, well-off thanks to this old family land, and still tied his thinning gray hair back in a ponytail and wore

Birkenstocks with white socks. During the strike at the piston factory a few years back, Dan had seen Ted on the sidewalk downtown. He'd come home for his mother's funeral. Dan drove by, pretending not to see Ted, not sure why he'd done it or why he felt a twinge of shame for doing it. There was just this yawning gulf between what they once meant to each other and what they were now. What they once were required a greeting and a "catching up." What they were now—Dan unemployed and Ted a trendy artist from San Diego—made that catching up unbearably awkward.

Ted, Dan, and Tom had also played their boyhood games in the wooded ravine that lay just beyond the Ballard farm's barn. Dan's mind flashed back to this afternoon and the ghost named Ellen. He sat replaying his encounter with her as an endless line of mini vans and SUVs filled with nameless families continued to exit the drive thru.

He finished his cheeseburger and found himself driving north down Main again, toward the Ballard farm. It was dark and the one headlight wobbled in the socket, oddly illuminating the under branches of trees as the truck rumbled ahead. The cool, damp night air rushed in the open window and whipped his hair about. Big Sandy and his Fly Rite Boys oozed from the CD player—a slow-dance, pedal steel guitar moaned a lonely twang out the truck windows, echoing off the houses that lined the street.

A quarter-mile beyond the crush of houses he made the banked curve in front of the Ballard farm but didn't pull into the drive. He looked at the house, barn, and the other outbuildings as he passed. All were dark. He half expected to see her somewhere, in a window or in the drive, but didn't.

Even though he saw nothing, he felt it. She was there. Ellen knew he was passing, and Dan knew it, somehow. He felt the same sensation he'd felt earlier today when he climbed the stairs, knowing without hearing or seeing that she was in the back room waiting for him. He went an eighth of a mile to the entrance of the old covered bridge with its park and walking trails and turned around.

Approaching in the opposite direction now, Dan slowed and pulled into the driveway. He didn't know why. Perhaps he wanted to be reassured that it had happened, that she had been here. During the day a feeling of dread had dogged him, but slowly that fear had dissipated. He wasn't afraid anymore, he was curious and oddly excited to have a secret so incredible all to himself. He turned off the truck and stepped into the grass, surveying the cozy space. It was perhaps fifty yards long and twenty-five yards wide, defined by trees along the road to the north, the meandering line of out buildings to the south, the house to the west end, the barn on the east.

Without an audible word Ellen spoke to him, *"Beyond the trees."*

There were trees in every direction, but Dan knew where she meant. There was a specific location in those three words that flashed in his mind. He knew she was beyond the trees behind the garage, or "carriage shed," as she had called it.

He walked cautiously along the side of the garage, tilting his head out to stretch his view and immediately saw her standing at the edge of the trees where a lane had once opened to a farm field, but now held the beginnings of Ballard Woods subdivision.

She smiled as he approached. "Yer not afraid," she said softly. "I'm surprised."

He didn't need to get any closer to read the expression on her face. In the dark, far from the lights of town, there was a faint illumination to her form that hadn't been noticeable in the upstairs room. Ellen's expression betrayed relief that he had come, and a hint of desperation at wanting his presence so badly. Again, information was in his mind without audible words. In fact what entered his mind did not come in the form of words at all, it was simply the understanding that this was a terribly lonely soul.

He stopped a few feet away from her with his hands in the pockets of his faded jeans and studied her gentle glow. The shadowed natural form you would expect from any shape in the dark was there in Ellen, the black and white tone of objects, the almost nonexistent contrast between fold and weave and texture. Yet, radiating above that natural appearance was a luminescence, an additional glimmering human fabric on top of the usual human form, as if Ellen were made of layers, the outermost glowing, yet transparent. The layers were distinct, yet intertwined in a way that was hard to define, like the fading of rainbow colors from one to another, iridescent like the wings of a starling caught in sunshine. The shimmering quality of the outer layer was subtle to the point of being far more captivating than a bold glow would have been, suggesting there were many more layers to be revealed. Dan found himself attracted to this being with the most compelling curiosity he had ever known in his life.

"Your glow ... is that what people have written about throughout history ... about ghosts?"

"I 'magine so. In a completely dark place it's 'bout all one can see."

"But you're not smoke or vapor, and I can't see through you."

Ellen turned away from him. "I suppose in any other set of circumstances such probing questions would be rude, but I understand why ya ask."

"I don't mean to offend you ... but these aren't normal circumstances."

"They are for me," she replied. "But, yes, I realize they are not normal for you. After all, I never once saw a ... ghost during my life. And now, since being ... spirit—I prefer to consider myself a spirit—I have only seen a few others besides myself."

Dan remained a short distance from her, but still too far back for proper polite conversation. Ellen sensed that there were remnants of fear in him yet. He was holding back, keeping her at more than arm's length. She turned back toward him, deciding to solve this once and for all.

"We might as well get this over with right now. You may come closer and see for yourself if ya like. I'm nothin' to be afraid of."

Dan wasn't really ready to come closer, but did, walking right up to her as he would any person, but with adrenaline accelerating his heart. He stood there in the darkness with the cool breeze washing across him and noticed that the loose strands of hair hanging alongside her face moved in the wind slightly out of sync as if on a separate plane that earthly wind could not touch. There was a feeling of electric anticipation as he looked at her and she at him, an emotional rush jumbling his ability to inspect her with the careful eye he wished to bring to the moment. He was trying to see everything at once and so had a hard time concentrating on anything in particular.

Up close she looked a little different than she had from afar, beyond improved clarity and the fact that, combined with the extra detail, her glow became less apparent. She really was a lovely woman.

She had an angular face with a strong, straight nose. Fine, young wrinkles spread from the outer corners of her eyes and around a mouth that had apparently smiled often. Her build was slight but strong and stood perhaps five foot six or seven. Dan pondered her age and guessed her to be in her midthirties.

"I was thirty-four when I died," Ellen said, interrupting his thoughts.

Narrowing his eyes on her, mouth agape, Dan asked, "Do you know everything I'm thinking?"

"No, but I often get flashes of meaning from the living, especially when their emotions run high ... when they're especially worked up."

They were silent a moment longer, watching one another's expressions.

"Why did ya come back tonight?" she asked.

Dan took a moment to answer, still examining her. Her chest fell and rose gently, just as that of a breathing, living being would. "Curiosity, I suppose."

"You must have many questions," she said. The comment seemed to have a purpose, to be more than awkward small talk.

Uneasy, Dan laughed, "About a thousand. But suddenly I can't think of one."

She didn't respond, but looked over her shoulder, out across the scarred open land. Lights from clusters of houses along the next road south, at the far end, twinkled like stars in the darkness.

"Walk with me, will you?" she asked.

Dan nodded. They walked slowly along the dirt roadway the earthmovers had made through the old cornfield. He was on her right, hands still in his pockets, his eyes drawn again, as they had been earlier in the day, to the fluid, unnatural, effortless way she moved.

"I understand yer wantin' to ask questions," she said, walking bolt upright, her hands at her sides. "But I have decided not to answer any more questions unless you agree to my terms."

"Which are?" Dan asked.

She stopped and faced him, speaking with a measured urgency in her voice. "For every question ya ask me, I may ask one of you. Total honesty is the only thing that will do. I promise I will tell ya nothin' but the truth and you must make the same pledge to me."

Dan was bewildered. "You don't owe me the right to ask any questions and I'm not sure I even want to," his voice rising. "And besides, why would you care about anything I could tell you? I don't know the answers to any mysteries of life."

"I don't want answers to the mysteries of life," Ellen said. "I want to know 'bout you and your life."

Dan's curiosity gave way to unease. He shook his head, pulled a hand from his pocket, and rubbed the back of his neck. "Why would you care about me?"

"I need a friend," she said emphatically. "I have been here more than a hundred and thirty-five years and I need a friend—someone to talk to!"

Dan walked on a few steps, not sure what to say. Ellen followed, watching the side of his face for a clue to his feelings. Dan shot a quick nervous glance at her and saw her concerned questioning expression. He stopped and faced her.

"So now you don't know what I'm thinking?"

She became self-conscious and shook her head.

"Probably 'cause I don't even know what I'm thinkin'," Dan mumbled to himself.

They walked on along the dirt roadway in silence, finally coming to new asphalt that had just been laid that day. Lingering warmth radiated upward. The petroleum-rich smell of tar was thick in the air. At the edges of the coarse black pavement were ribbons of white concrete curbs stretching out across the land in gentle curves. Parked here and there in the dirt alongside the brand new streets were the yellow earthmovers.

"We could talk each day when ya come to do yer work," Ellen said finally, breaking the silence.

"Who's to say I'm coming back?" Dan grunted.

"You have to. You don't have a choice."

"How do you know that?" Dan asked, stopping again and turning to her.

"In the barn the other day, when I scared ya, yer fear was intense enough I could read the reason you stayed. You need the money yer gettin' from the things yer takin' from the house. Yer poor." Her voice trailed off as she belatedly tried to stop herself from saying those words.

Those two words stung Dan's pride. The embarrassment was intense enough that she read that, too. He hadn't been poor his whole life. Not until now. She hadn't told him anything he didn't already know. Even so, the anger born of shame remained.

"Yes, I do need to come back here 'till I get it all, everything of value," he said abruptly.

"Why are you poor?" she asked, searchingly, with an almost childlike innocence, immediately ignoring that she had offended him and driving ahead anyway to satisfy her curiosity.

Dan's expression turned hard, "Well, I don't know," he spat, "why are you dead?"

As soon as he said it, he wished he hadn't.

Ellen jerked her head back in surprise. Her face tightened, her eyes intense. "Childbirth," she whispered.

"What?" Dan breathed, surprised she'd even attempted to answer his cruel rhetorical question.

"Childbirth," she repeated, only a little louder, stung now a little herself.

"Aw hell," Dan smirked, shaking his head and rubbing his neck again, exasperated with himself and this ridiculous situation. "I'm sorry I even came back here tonight." He turned and started walking quickly back toward his truck.

Ellen faded out, then reappeared some ten feet in front of him. Dan caught sight of her just in time to jump a step to the left in surprise, but didn't stop.

"Please," she begged, as he walked by, "don't go! I didn't mean to offend you."

He continued on. Ellen kept pace alongside him. "Please stop and just hear me out. Please!"

Dan couldn't help but be distracted again by the elegant way she moved at this speed, not walking in measured movements, but hurrying in her half-walking, half-floating gait. He stopped with his hand on the door handle of the truck and looked back at her. He couldn't be mean to this woman ... this spirit. His heart was awash with curiosity, sympathy, and fear—not fear of a ghost, but fear of intimacy, fear of telling someone how he'd ended up in this place in his life.

"I'll be back in the morning to continue my salvage work," Dan said, not wanting to appear to be giving in, "and if you got questions, well you can go ahead and ask 'em."

He got in his truck and pulled the door closed.

"Thank you," Ellen said.

"And this fading in and out business ... you're not going to appear at my house someday are you?"

"I can't," she said.

"No offense," Dan said, "but ... good!"

He started the engine but reconsidered and quickly turned it off. "Well, here's my first real question," he said. "Why can't you do that?"

"I don't know," Ellen said. "When I get to the edge of the farm, I can feel myself ... my form ... my being coming apart ... being drawn away. So I don't go on. It's terrifying."

He began to start the truck again, but she raised her palm and stepped closer. "My response question—I see your wedding ring—your wife, what's her name?"

"I'm divorced. Her name was ... is, Sue.

"I'm sorry."

"Yeah, me, too."

CHAPTER 5

Dan felt Ellen's presence. From the moment his truck made the tight, banked curve in front of the house that morning he knew she was there.

He parked in the empty yard and looked through the opening of trees to the earthmovers and the construction crew setting forms for the foundation of a house far to the southern end of the farm. Now that the entrance road was paved to the south, the crews parked nearer their work, leaving the driveway and overgrown yard before the grouping of old buildings empty and silent but for the tittering and peeping of birds in the trees.

He set up the ladder and slipped on a tool belt, anticipating her appearance, but she did not come. Climbing the ladder he picked up where he'd left off the day before, but she did not speak or peer from a window. He worked all morning until he thought he'd go mad with curiosity.

At lunchtime he walked the rooms of the empty house. There was no sign, just the nagging sensation he could not define that told him she was nearby. As he sat on the tailgate eating a bologna sandwich Dan committed to forcing her from his mind. As the afternoon wore on, he thought of his daughter and Sue and tried to estimate the value of all the salvage.

Finally in midafternoon she appeared at the base of his ladder. He didn't see her until her voice spoke out a sentence that startled him and set his heart beating from the shock.

"Lovely day for working," Ellen said.

Dan looked down at her in surprise, putting his hand to his heart as if to calm it. She smiled up at him. Wasting no time, she asked, "Do you have a question ready?"

Her query was loaded with suggestions. The obvious questions dealt with death and the hereafter. Not his style. Dan had already settled on never asking such questions directly, but to let it dribble out, perhaps ask about something else that would lead there. So, instead of asking about death, he quickly went to the opposite end of the spectrum. "Where were you born? Your accent is a little Hoosier, and a little not."

"I was born in Kentucky," she said, "south of Lexington. Lived there 'til I was 'bout six. Don't remember much about it. My father said the bit of land we had was no good. It's the journey I remember ... bits and pieces ... splinters of memory." She fell silent, as if conjuring up the mental picture.

Dan stood beneath his work at the top of the ladder, the deep eaves jutting out over his head. He wanted to say something, to try and act calm, to hide his nervousness. He scratched the tip of his chin with the claw of the hammer. "People around here like to make fun of Kentucky ... feel like they're better than people from down there. If they think you're backward or less worldly or something, they'll call your town, 'Muncie-tucky,' or 'Tipton-tucky,' or make inbreeding jokes, like everybody from Kentucky is a hillbilly or something."

She didn't look at him or change expression in any measurable way, but she was considering what he said.

"Well, such ... self-righteous Hoosiers would be surprised at how many of their ancestors come from Kentucky. When I was growin' up 'round here, there were lots of folks from Kentucky callin' this town," she nodded south, "home."

Dan felt her defensiveness. "I guess it takes a lot of gall for Hoosiers to think they're better than Kentuckians."

He turned back to his work, beginning to wedge the pry bar into the seam of cracked paint between the fascia board and bracket.

A feeling overtook him slowly, with a depth of meaning that, though simple, was strikingly unique, like but a few intuitive understandings he'd ever had with another person. It was gentle reproach. She had wanted to tell him something but he had drawn the conversation away toward small talk.

Dan looked down, ready to apologize. Instead he puzzled over the apron tied around her waist. *There is no work for her to do in this house—and what would she do if there was?* he thought to himself. But he abruptly stifled the thought, fearing she would read it.

She sat on the stump of a tree, legs crossed beneath her dress, elbow on her knee, chin in her hand. She was waiting, waiting to pick up where she'd left off before he interrupted with his nonsense about Kentuckians and Hoosiers.

"The journey ..." he prompted, "you were going to say something about the journey."

She began again.

"We came up toward Richmond, through southern Indiana to the National Road, made our way to Indianapolis and then willy-nilly up this way. I remember crossin' the Ohio on a ferry—I was excited and terrified, both at once! I'd never seen a piece of water so big in my life. I remember walkin' and ridin' for three days straight in the most terrible dashes of rain you ever saw. During this time ... along some swollen stream, they took the wheels off the wagons and tied logs to the underneath and pulled 'em—floated 'em across the water. Me and Mama laid on our bellies with our eyes closed almost all the way across."

She smiled and turned wistful, "Do you have a really early memory, so early but clear, like a perfect picture painted in yer mind, you can relive it again and again? This is one of mine: I can still remember my view, layin' there with my cheek to a wet plank. If I strained my eyes up I could see the choppy water and the muddy bank ahead. If I strained them down I saw the same thing receding. Straight ahead, just inches from my face was Mama lookin' back at me and with my tiny brother, Isiah, wrapped in her arms. She was frantic, angry at my father's impatience, forcin' us across the water that way. Wiry strands of stray hair from her bun hung down in her face. She cried, 'O goodness Ellen! We're gonna die.'

"I hadn't had sense enough to be afraid ... trusted in the wisdom of adults, 'till she said that. Then I cried 'till we got to the other side. It's funny, as scary as it was, I'd go back to that moment right now if I could to see her face again, to feel that fear, that passionate fear that a child feels ... and to see my mama again."

Dan stopped working a time or two and gazed down from the ladder, listening to her slow measured tone, trying to catch her expression, but couldn't see her face much at all.

She was looking out across the land at the trees and barn and grain house as she spoke.

"Mama hated the trip, didn't wanna go in the first place," she said, speaking more quickly, "but Papa insisted, said it would be all easy pickin's in Indiana. Kentucky had apparently been bad, but it was a bad she knew. 'Better the devil ya know than the one ya don't know,' she liked to say. When we got to the land Papa picked out, north of here a couple miles, Mama just fell into sobs. It was swampy, covered with trees. It was nothin' like he said it would be.

"He sold most everything we had in Kentucky to buy that piece of land, sight unseen. All along the trip, every time my mama would start to complain or say he'd made a mistake, he'd build that place up to be better and better, sayin' 'You're gonna love it up in Indiana, the land is rich and flat—it'll be the easiest we ever had it.' He sure was wrong, at first anyway.

"I can still see her walking about when we set up camp there, tending a fire and making a dinner for us. She just cried and cried and cried, stirring a pot with one hand and cradling Isiah against her breast with the other. Even though I was only small, I could see the terrible contradiction in her. The tears were the childish tears of a crybaby and the cooking and tending to things was the hard-working resignation of a grown woman.

"It was nothin' like he said it would be. Guess sometimes men make foolish choices," she said.

There was a long pause. Dan was hesitant to interrupt the story but felt moved to comment. "Maybe her working while she was so upset was her way of getting through the moment. She was a mother and a wife, she knew how to cook and care for children ... so she did it even though she was so upset ... or maybe *because* she was so upset. It was a way of giving a piece of order to a situation that was terribly out of order. Besides, it needed doing."

Dan was surprised to hear these words come from his own mouth, but it felt right to say. He sensed it and felt that Ellen would appreciate the comment. "Your mama did the only thing she knew how to do."

He stepped halfway down the ladder, gripping the side rail with the fingertips of his left hand, which also held a hammer. He bent low and gently dropped a heavy bracket in the yard and saw that Ellen had stood and was watching him with interest.

She smiled up at him. "Yes, I guess she did what she had to do."

"It all worked out?" he asked, climbing back up.

Ellen rested her hand on the back of her hips and arched her back gently as if it ached, stepping into the shade of a hackberry. "They cut down some trees to make a cabin on the driest piece of ground they could find and then set to drainin' the land and takin' down trees.

"Those early years were hard, but once a good bit of land was cleared, oh, you wouldn't believe how rich and black that soil was my daddy would turn up on that old swamp land. It could grow crops like magic.

"The town," she nodded south, "wasn't much more than a dirty crossroad when we got here. By the time I died it was a busy place with a railway station and mills down by the river. Seeing what's happening here," she nodded south again toward the work crews beyond the trees, "I can only imagine what it's like now?"

Dan pulled loose another bracket and headed back down the ladder. Ellen watched him descend, thinking perhaps he was more interested in his work than her story, but when he got to the bottom and dropped the bracket he said, "If you got in my truck and drove the country roads along the farms ... well there aren't many fields left south of here ... but north of here ... in the springtime, after plowing, you'd see that the soil is just as black and rich as ever—going right into Tipton County—but I heard there were lots of swamps up there too—so it makes sense. Eons of decayed plant matter all stacked up underfoot."

Dan was moved by her story. The idea of what this land once was intrigued him. Moving the Indians off—it was wrong; he knew that, but still, once they were gone, if you thought of it from just that moment—it was like the land was a blank slate for the settlers, even the second wave of settlers like Ellen's family. That blank slate ... what could you do with it that would make it all turn out differently—different than the winding streets and the bulldozers and the retention ponds and the vinyl siding and the matching mailboxes and the strip malls and fast food and all the rest?

Ellen's eyes met his as he dropped the bracket alongside the others. She looked suddenly pained and her nostrils flared slightly and to Dan she looked almost like a real person as she spoke:

"I ... I don't know what to think of all that," she said, searchingly, shaking her head, "the Indians and the ... bull-dozers?" she motioned beyond the milk house toward the subdivision going up.

She emphatically crossed her hands on her chest and said simply, "If I have a story to tell, then the Indians ... and the bulldozers ... are my bookends. I have no direct connection to either, but they bind my world at either end.

"As a child we gathered and kept the arrowheads and axe

heads that were churned up by the plowing and wondered at these missing, invisible people and the remains of their world, their tools. And here I am watching these yellow machines with no more understanding of them than I had for the Indians."

Dan stood watching her speak, a hammer in one hand and a pry bar in the other, knowing she had read the thought he meant to keep to himself and then responded to it, unasked. To have his thoughts so naked was both magnificent and terrifying at the same time, liberating in a way that felt like relief.

Reading again, she took a step closer to him, her hands still crossed on her chest, but her voice softer and less urgent, "If you don't want me to know what you're feelin' then you will have to guard your feelings better. I don't want not to know what you're feelin', but then, I don't wantcha to feel ... overly exposed." She started to turn away but then quickly turned back. "Is it eavesdropping if it just comes to you like the wind, unasked for?"

Dan stood, tools in hand, looking at her, considering the insanity of the moment and trying to digest it. He tried not to think anything—and everything—think chaos even. It worked. As he moved the ladder between the next two brackets, she moved around him.

"We haven't lived up to our agreement very well, have we?" she prodded, hoping to open his mind back up.

"What do you mean?"

"One may ask one question in return for each question asked."

"I ain't upset," he said, kicking the two side rails of the ladder into the dirt with the heels of his boot, trying to act uninterested, "life don't happen in sound bites."

Ellen considered the term. "Small talk ... short, simple answers—that's whatcha mean by sound bites?"

"Yeah, life don't work that way, does it? At least it shouldn't."

"Not usually," she agreed, walking now with her hands behind her back, watching him climb the ladder from the corner of her eye. The mental chaos was working and it irritated her. She could never read it all, and sometimes only glean bits of useful or defining information. In her current state she had only once before gone this far, this openly, with a living being. The fear of her initial presence had always triggered emotions high enough to read in others before. But she had given Dan the truth about what she was, and more time to grow at ease with it.

"But the essence, the underlying meaning of the agreement—'tit for tat,' that must not be ignored, right?" she asked.

Dan didn't answer. As he climbed the ladder and poked at the next bracket, he gave Ellen the same silent treatment he always gave Sue when she was looking for his emotions. But he'd made an agreement with this being, one he felt compelled to live up to. With Sue the silent treatment was his final statement on the issue, a stone wall that could not be moved. But now, somehow, it was simply a stalling tactic, allowing him to gather his thoughts.

It was his turn to reciprocate, to share a piece of himself. Then it came: a question asked without speaking, *"Where were you born?"*

Two stories up again, he gripped the side rails of the ladder with either hand, squeezed his eyes shut, forced the mental chaos away and refocused.

"I was born in this town," he said, tentatively, as if being questioned by the police, "forty-eight years ago."

Ellen sat back down, satisfied that he would do as he had agreed to.

Dan lifted the pry bar and hammer from his tool belt and began working around another bracket. "The town it was then ... fifty years ago ... if you had seen it, would have been as foreign to you as it is to me now. What were the boundaries then—in your day?"

"Oh, Wayne Street to the north, Pleasant Street to the south, the river to the west, and Floyd to the east," she replied.

"Well, that was still the core—when I was born, but it had grown a lot, and now, well, there's been an explosion of growth, and you can see right over there where it's going.

"When my wife ... ex ... wife and I were young and talking about having kids we talked a lot about living someplace else, moving out west or down south, but we never did. When the discussion would get around to what kind of place we wanted our kids to grow up in ... well ... we just couldn't think of anything better than here, the upbringing we had. It was a good place to raise kids.

"One summer when I was a kid my father drove me out Route 66, out west. I got memories from that trip that are like your childhood journey up here—visions in my mind so crisp and clear—like they happened yesterday. I saw so many things, so many places I'd only read about in books and seen in movies. There were beautiful mountains ... I mean, hell, I grew up in Indiana—what did I know about mountains. I saw cities—big cities! I saw it all—that great big hunk of land that you think of when you hear that song, 'This land is your land, this land is my land, from California,' ... and I wasn't afraid of it or put off by it or threatened in any way. I was thrilled that my dad had taken me to see it all. But still ... on the trip home ... first when the land flattened, then when the plains gave way to fields dotted with woods and then when we hit central Illinois and then turned off

66 and came to the Indiana border—bit by bit I felt more and more at home—like I was returning to ... civilization. It ain't like I think Indiana's better than any place else ... but it's *my* place. Towns with a courthouse in the middle and tall brick buildings all around ... and houses beyond that and corn fields and woods beyond that."

Dan's mind replayed what he'd just said and he got a fleeting glimpse of the cultural references Ellen likely had no knowledge of. "Does that make sense to you?" he asked.

"I don't understand the particulars of everything you said, but I think I feel and understand the meaning."

Dan pulled loose the last bracket and cradled it on the top rung as he slipped the hammer and pry bar into the tool belt. He turned around to look at Ellen and almost didn't see her, she was standing in bright sunlight now and was nearly transparent, not like smoke or mist, but more like she were made of water or glass. Tiny beams of light occasionally pierced the edges of her form and splintered, as if through a prism, like tinsel blown through a flashlight's beam. She was standing in the tall grass beside the red brick house, her open palm to her forehead like a salute, shielding her eyes from the sun. It was the first time he'd seen her in brilliant, direct sunlight and again, like seeing her in the dark, she was beautiful, like a rare, exotic animal, captivating in a way that made it hard not to look, hard not to wonder about the mysteries she was made of.

"What's yer favorite color?" Ellen asked, looking up at him.

He thought hard for a minute. "I haven't been asked that question since my kids were small." From his perch high above the ground he could see the deep green corn leaves swaying across the road. "Green, I 'spect. And yours?"

"Blue," she said quickly, her answer given so fast it seemed to Dan that she'd asked him his only so she could tell him hers. As he climbed down the ladder she walked past and moved into the shade, recapturing normal opacity, again looking almost alive.

"I really did want to know," she said, "but I've always known mine and I'm proud of it—sky blue, like a robin's egg."

"You chose the sky and I chose the earth ... fitting somehow," Dan said, gathering up the last armload of brackets before heading to the truck.

That feeling again!

Like a tingling wave of electricity it washed through his body. As he moved through the grass he could feel the hair stand up on the back of his neck and sensed again immediately that she was hurt by his casual comment ... and the why of it struck him like a bolt of lightning. Suddenly she was in front of him, standing near the truck.

"Is this why you and your wife are divorced?" she snapped.

Dan's jaw was set tight in defense. "Is what why?" he asked, moving past her and stacking the brackets in the back of the truck.

"That you would say such a ... hurtful thing. I know what ya meant—you belong to the earth 'cause yer alive and I belong to the sky because I'm dead."

"How is that a surprise to you?" Dan asked dismissively.

"It's ... it's not a surprise to me," she stammered, "but just because it's true don't mean ya have to shove it in my face. If a woman is ugly, is it right to say it out loud just because she must already know it?"

Dan dropped the last of the brackets on the tailgate and gestured with open palms toward her, "I wasn't trying to throw it in your face ..."

Ellen interrupted with a pleading whine, "Well you did." She stepped a few feet away, then turned sharply back, teeth clenched, shaking her finger at the ground, "You have no idea how difficult it is to be in this state ... in limbo ... neither here nor there, unable to go backward—unable to go forward ... and worst of all bein' 'round to see everything that says who ya are bein' ripped apart ... and not bein' able to do anything about it."

Dan hesitated, taking in the fury in her eyes. He was mad, mad at being lectured about things he knew all too well himself. "Sometimes being alive ain't any different," he said.

With that she closed her eyes, pursed her lips in disappointment, and disappeared.

Dan looked about the yard, looking for her to reappear. Nothing.

In a sudden bolt Tom's black Hummer bounded across the front yard. Dan sighed in exasperation.

"Bone-sure, man-sewer," Tom quipped in mock-French from the open window, flashing a bright white smile, "how ya doin'?"

"Fine," Dan replied, irritated at Tom's bad timing. He went on with his loading.

"Has our mystery lady made any more appearances?"

"Nope, all's quiet here."

"Guess nail'n things shut did the trick."

"Guess so."

"Well, gotta go," he said, slapping his palm on the car door. "See ya 'round if ya don't turn square."

Dan forced a smile and waved. Tom shot out the driveway and down the eastern curve toward the covered bridge.

Dan quickly shoved the last of the brackets forward, slammed the tailgate shut, and got into the truck. He didn't want Ellen to reappear—didn't know what he'd say to her if she did.

CHAPTER 6

When Dan pulled onto 15th Street he saw Kristin's Honda parked in the driveway. Once through the door he found she'd cleaned the whole apartment and was cooking at the stove.

She turned and smiled broadly. "Daddy," she said, and came to him and hugged him, wrapping her arms around his neck. She purposefully rubbed her cheek against his whiskers as she'd done since she was a small child. The cheerless mood Ellen had left him in evaporated.

"This is a surprise," he said, pulling back to look into her face.

"Thought you could use a little female help around here."

"This is a pretty solitary place," he smirked, embarrassed by his apartment, feeling like a disobedient child. She hugged her father tight again and held him longer than seemed normal. He wondered if something was wrong.

Since the day she was born, Dan said Kristin was a gift from God. As an infant she seldom cried and in childhood grew into a tiny angel. She was loving, obedient, clever, and beautiful. As a teenager she was mature beyond her years, not physically, but intellectually and emotionally, "sixteen going on thirty-five," Dan always said when people at the factory asked, "How's your girl?"

Kristin wore blue jeans, a plain white T-shirt, and leather strap sandals. She was twenty-two years old, freshly graduated from Indiana University and done with a summer session of graduate courses. She had shoulder length blonde hair and a nice, though unremarkable, figure. Her self-conscious smile reminded Dan of his mother ... and her mother. She was a pleasant contradiction; a go-getter who knew how to solve problems, but soft spoken and gentle in the way she went about it—a Hoosier to the core. Her quiet determination made for many pleasant surprises, for her hard work took place so inconspicuously that the final accomplishment was often unexpected.

As a child she spoke with a lisp. At age three it was unbearably cute, but by age seven was a source of embarrassment for her. Though it was near completely trained away in speech therapy classes, there was a faint hint of it yet in her voice, as if she weren't entirely in control of the muscles that formed her words. Dan always thought that if Kristin were a singer she'd sound like Billie Holiday, or Ricki Lee Jones.

She pulled back and brushed paint chips from his hair. "Well, why don't you go take a shower and I'll finish dinner. Wanna beer?"

Kristin got him a Budweiser from the refrigerator and he disappeared into the bathroom. She went on sipping from her own bottle and stirring a pot of spaghetti sauce while the shower hissed in the next room.

From the shower he heard Jason Isbell's pleading tenor singing a truck driver's lonely confession. Kristin was playing music she knew he liked. Isbell's recovered hell-raiser persona spoke to Dan, and she knew it. Water splattered on his face as the descending chords of the chorus calmed his troubled mind.

It was upsetting to be with him this way in this place. Every time she came home from college she dealt anew with his absence from the little house on 16th Street where she and her brother grew up. He should be there with her mother, but he wasn't—what the mind knows but the heart cannot accept. And then to find him here in this little ramshackle apartment. It was hard. The alt-country music and the beer were the only touchstones that connected those two worlds— not nearly enough to settle her unsettled heart.

Still, she smiled and tried to act as if nothing was out of the ordinary. She had committed to herself to stay with him here this time instead of with her mother at the house. It would be awkward, she suspected. Her mother told her it would be. But then Kristin didn't need to talk as much as her mother did and so her relationship with her father was made much easier. Still, she was a woman; a quiet woman and a quiet man are never completely in tune.

"Thank you, Daddy," she said later, passing him the garlic bread across the little table in the kitchen.

"Thank you for what?"

"Thank you for saving so well for my college. It's been so much easier for me not to have to hold down two jobs or drop out for semesters to work like some of my friends have to do. And to not have mountains of college loans ... thank you. You and Mom did alright by me and Mark."

Dan just smiled and went on arranging food on his plate. "You say that every time you come home and every time it's completely unnecessary."

"Thank you, Daddy," she said again.

He just smiled and nodded his head gently up and down, a mouth full of food.

"So how are things down in Bloomington?" he asked, wiping his mouth with a paper napkin."

"Booming-town, just like here. Sometimes I think it'd be nice to live someplace where everything isn't constantly in upheaval."

"Some people like to complain about it," Dan said, "but it's sure made this town rich. That's not so bad."

"You don't really think that, Daddy?"

"What do you mean I don't think that. I said it, didn't I?"

"You say it because you're supposed to say it ... because everybody else around here says it. Everybody else says it because it puts money in their pockets, but I don't believe you really feel it. You can say it, but you don't really think that. You're just being the good Hoosier who never questions progress."

Dan didn't answer, but went on eating, looking down at his plate.

"The growth and change hasn't helped you any," she said.

She'd been looking at him, but after lobbing that last comment, fell silent, looked down at her own plate, and went about eating in a more defensive posture.

"The growth and change didn't make the Japanese buy the factory," he grunted, still not looking up at her.

"Yeah, but it sure made your hometown unrecognizable and turned your friends into ... different people," she finished uncertainly, wishing she'd found a more specific way to say it.

"Nothin' lasts forever," Dan said.

"Aarrgh! You say that just to dismiss the point, but you don't really feel that way. Please, tell me you don't feel that way."

"You sayin' that I think things last forever?"

She took a breath. "You know what I'm saying," she answered softly, "I'm saying that sometimes it's sad for things to change the way they do, and just because something's new doesn't make it good."

He smiled at her uncommon insistence, "You're really full of piss and vinegar tonight, aren't ya?"

She smiled back and let it go. He'd heard her point and she knew it. She didn't need to hear him admit it.

"Well, know something that does piss me off?" he asked. "Fuckin' Belgians bought Budweiser. How's that shit for ya? Budweiser's made by Europeans now. Doesn't anything stay the same?"

He winked, took a sip of his beer, and gave her the beer bottle salute, tilting the bottle toward her.

"And your secret war on pop country music? How's that going?"

"Aw come on," he grimaced, tilting his head in challenge, "you hate pop-country as much as I do ... all those young, pretty blonde fakes—like FOX News anchors, and pretty boys in their tight jeans and cowboy hats and contrived songs about trucks and small towns and ... shit, drinkin' and pretty girls. How fuckin' fake!"

"Everybody can't be Steve Earle, Daddy."

"They don't have to be," he insisted, reciting a tired old line she'd heard a hundred times, "just be who you are. Tell your story, and don't worry 'bout what the record company wants. Don't sell your soul chasing an audience, do your thing and let the audience find you! Nashville is a corporate hell hole. They crank out music same way Apple makes phones in China, on an assembly line."

"You're preaching to the choir, Daddy."

Dan smiled and took another sip of beer, "I like having you in my choir," he saluted again.

They ate in silence for several minutes.

"This house you're salvaging ... anything interesting?"

Dan rolled a forkful of pasta and sauce in his mouth as he searched for an answer that might strike a balance between reality and honesty. Instead, he settled as he always did, with benign evasion, "There're some things there that are worth money. It's just an old house. Nothin' special," he finally lied.

"I see you've got a pile of stuff ... an old porch out back and a truckload of gingerbread today. Good money?"

"Thousand bucks, maybe," Dan mumbled through a mouthful of bread. He chewed quickly, trying to down the rest and ask a question before she had time to quiz him more about the Ballard farm. He felt uneasy revealing any more than he had to.

"So what's next for you, Sugarcube?"

Kristin crossed her legs and smiled her self-conscious smile at being called by his childhood nickname for her. She knew he meant it with love, but now it made her feel inferior—smaller—like a child. "I don't know, Daddy."

"Hard to let go of the carefree years, ain't it?"

"Oh, really, it's nothing so petty as that. I like Blooming-ton, I like it a lot. Mostly I like to learn ... you know that," she finished, a hint of pleading in her voice. "I'm torn. I don't really belong there anymore. I see these eighteen-year-old freshmen coming in and acting like such fools and it makes me feel old. You know what I mean?" she laughed nervously.

"Oh yeah, I know what you mean," he chuckled, "watched it in the factory more than I'd like to remember."

"They'll flirt with me in a bar or the library and I'm thinking, 'Oh sure,'" she laughed, covering her mouth with her palm and then gesturing openly, shaking her head to the ceiling, "like I'm interested in little boys like you."

"So why are you still there?"

She took a long draw from her beer and smirked at him, "It's hard to let go of the carefree years?"

Dan grinned broadly back at her.

"But it's hard to know what I'm avoiding ... leaving where I am ... or moving on to the next step in life."

"A job?"

She shrugged her shoulders, her pale cheeks warmed and rosy from a third beer.

They finished their dinner in silence and worked together cleaning up before settling in front of a couple movies Kristin had downloaded on her laptop. She went on during the first one, telling her father what to watch for, what she liked, why it was such a good movie, before falling asleep during the second movie, the one she'd downloaded thinking he would like it.

She lay asleep on the couch. Dan sat on the Lazy Boy, uninterested in the movie, nursing another beer, and replaying his conversations today with Ellen and Kristin.

His thoughts and emotions were laid bare by the alcohol and his weariness and these strange encounters with a spirit, the vibes from a ghost changing his being somehow. Dan thought to himself that he might open up to Kristin, now, at this moment, if she were awake. Tonight, Kristin had been digging for some purer expression of his feelings, for advice even, but he had kept his usual distance. He would change that now if she were awake.

She needed for him to explain the last several years. Just as she was becoming mature and aware enough to care about and understand her parents' marriage, it fell apart. She was now preparing to spread her own wings and really leave home and take on the life of an adult and somehow, for it to feel right, she needed to know that they were there together and that everything at home base was secure and normal, but it wasn't. She wanted to know why and he knew this. She wasn't even sure of the direction she should take and she wanted her father's help, but he had remained merely friendly, unreachable, in his usual jovial way. She needed for him to open up, to share his wisdom, to reveal himself, and he knew he needed to do it, too. If she had been awake, he might have done it for real.

He formed the words and forced them out.

"Does it seem odd," Dan asked, hoarsely, "staying here in this place with your dad? Your mom's place has been your place since you came home from the hospital twenty-two years ago. It's been your home, your room, your place for as long as you can remember. And now here you are, staying with me. You've come home, but you're not quite home ... things aren't quite right, but you're here just the same, going through the motions."

Kristin went on sleeping. Dan smiled at the sight of her face crumpled against the couch cushion. "I love you, Kristin," he said, only the walls and the droning from the laptop to hear.

Leaving the movie running, Dan slipped out the front door, locking it behind him. He started his truck and headed north on Main.

CHAPTER 7

The night was still in the yard and drive, that peaceful courtyard like space, sheltered by the house and outbuildings and
trees. It was near completely dark. Shooting glances around
the edges of the buildings, he forced his hands into his
pockets and moved toward the barn. The grass hissed softly
as his worn leather work boots waded through the thick,
overgrown blades topped with heavy, bobbing seed tassels.
Here and there the stock of a volunteer redbud snapped under
foot. The gentle chorus of crickets nearest him quieted as he
walked in slow measured steps. No sign of her.

Finally, before the monolithic face of the barn and its
double doors, he stopped straining his eyes against the
darkness and closed them tight. He tried to clear his mind
of all thoughts except ... apology. Almost as soon as he had,
she spoke to him: *"Delicate things must be carefully kept."*

He immediately moved toward the trees behind the carriage shed, walking along the narrow path between the grain house and the tangled mass of trees and shrubs. She was there in the clearing just as she had been the night before, her back to him. He stood watching her softly shimmering in the darkness.

The feeling of her apology meeting his came without words—just meaning. Again, but more powerful than before, the arrival of pure understanding passed like a spiritual convulsion within him, coming up through his stomach and filling and expanding his chest and then his head like the rush of a powerful and intoxicating drug, clearing his sinuses like a cold blast of camphor. His sense of hearing left him for a moment as the sensation seemed to work its way right on out the top of his head, leaving his ears tingling and eyes watering. Through it all Dan saw her mouth opened wide, as if she were taking in a sharp breath at a moment of wonder. And she had crossed her arms on her chest as it swelled with the same heavenly emotion, not in the act of sending it, but of feeling it in unison with him.

He stood speechless, breathing heavily, watching the faint light from a sliver of moon catch and flow with the glow of the side of her face.

Just as stillness was returning to his senses, the most pure and seamless image appeared in his mind. It was a memory filled with earthly, bodily smells, sounds of muffled conversation and heavy, erratic breathing and the feeling of cold on the face and hands and the taste of sweat on the tongue.

But this was not his memory.

A multipaned window covered on the inside with frost gathered the flicker of gentle firelight that danced on flowered wallpaper all around. The clarity of the surroundings was obscured by a few strands of hair and the misty nature of perception caught at the edges of exhaustion. But these were the expressive parts of the vision. The vision was also filled with a torrent of emotions: dread, fear, release, joy.

There was nothing unclear or misunderstood about this multidimensional vision. He knew it took place here, in the house, in the front upstairs bedroom, where Ellen had been standing when she shouted at him, when he encountered her for the first time.

The vision was interrupted by the sound of Ellen's gentle voice:

"My first child was born on a very cold winter night in 1854," she said, turning to him. She said nothing more for a few minutes, just giving Dan time to gather his senses.

"The doctor could not make it in time. The snow was thick. We delivered it here," she nodded toward the house, "just my husband, his mother, and ... of course, me.

"I was so lucky to have the sort of mother-in-law I got. Most young wives had a mother-in-law they couldn't stand. That's the age-old story I guess. But I was so lucky to have mine live on with me ... beyond me. After I died she acted as mother to my children, even after my husband remarried. And it all began on that cold January night. She was lovin' and patient, supportive and generous. I mighta lost my mind that night if it weren't for her. I had a little girl. Beaul.

"Death is odd. There's so much you cannot take, but I have sight, hearing ... and smell. Whatever it is about the sense of smell, whatever the natural components—I can re-create them for myself, and the most captivatin' smell of all is that of a baby's breath, sloppy wet with her mother's milk."

She closed her eyes and seemed to strain outward. Suddenly Dan was greeted with that wonderful smell he remembered from baby Mark more than twenty-four years before and baby Kristin two years later.

"It is a brief thing for any parent I guess, a few months when you can smell it anytime you like, bendin' over the rails of a crib in the middle of the night to hear the breathin' ... watch the little chest rise and fall ... just to assure yourself. And then that gentle aroma that greets you, speakin' of precious, new life. And then there are the long stretches of years when you would give anything to smell it again, strain at yourself to remember it. Every time I held someone else's baby, at church, or visitin', I'd get a tiny scent of it and it would send me yearnin' for another baby of my own."

Ellen turned back over her shoulder to look at him and smiled. She nodded toward the wood and started walking. Dan followed.

He walked beside her, watching her radiance in the surrounding darkness. The night was terribly dark, but he followed easily. In the knee-deep grass, halfway to the line of trees, Ellen unexpectedly stopped and crossed her arms on her chest again and another memory swept through his mind, filling him with the sense of another moment not entirely unlike the first she had shared with him moments earlier.

Though his eyes were closed, they were overcome by intense light coming through the multipaned window. His mind's eye adjusted. The same room, the one from which she had first yelled at him while he stood working on the ladder, filled with morning sunlight. It was hot, terribly hot. The doctor and mother-in-law soothed and cooed in gentle tones. There was sweat and heat, so much, like on the hottest of summer days during the hardest of work when you stop caring, stop noticing that you're drenched. This time the wash of pain was intense, but less frightening, and then the gradual mounting of pressure and pain, the salty taste of sweat on his tongue. Finally, mercifully, the end was more like reward than relief—this time. The winter vision she had shared earlier was a snapshot of a moment, but this vision held perhaps hours of time within just minutes, still it was seamless and pure. It ended with laughter and exhilaration, and then a crying baby raised up, then laid on a towel upon her chest, bloody and wet.

This time Dan had more of his wits about him and was lost in the experience of reliving the birth with her. He was examining the baby, feeling a depth of emotion that was like a euphoria-inducing drug—to see it and feel it anew, dropped into the moment instead of experiencing the moment as the end result of a progression of events in his own life.

He was drawn out of the moment by pressure on his arm. He opened his eyes, adjusting now to the bewildering darkness of the meadow and this cooler, dryer reality.

He focused in on her face, looking back at him with a sort of surprised joy. Surprised, that he was so moved by the vision—joy, that it mattered now to someone else—the birth of a child, a child now long ago grown to a man and then dead at old age.

"We named him James," she said smiling, gripping Dan's arm, trying to wake him.

Whatever she was now, physically, whatever it was that made up her being, did not feel to the touch like another human, but was instead a gentle pinch of pressure and a faint tingle of electricity—like a pinched nerve.

"His name was James, and he was an absolute angel," she said, smiling.

Though he was not crying, Dan's eyes were misty. The raw wash of emotions he had just experienced was simply more intense than anything he could recall feeling. It had cracked open something inside and left him feeling on the edge—the edge between the usual facade he showed the world and some other person inside of himself he didn't know how to deal with.

Ellen's expression of joy turned to curiosity and she studied his face and the emotion that radiated from him. She saw the boundaries, it was time to ease up, let him catch his breath.

He felt a tug at his arm again. They continued on through the tall grass toward the woods. "Delicate things must be carefully kept," Dan said hoarsely, repeating her initial mental suggestion. "What things?"

"I was never taken very seriously in my home, as a child. Boys are taken seriously, not girls. But I had strong opinions and wanted to be heard, which my father had little patience for. I suppose that out of that upbringin' I became a little defensive ... a little prickly about bein' respected.

"After I got married, my new home here," she nodded back toward the farm buildings as they entered the woods, "was completely different. My husband, his brother, and their mother—they were *real* Christians.

"Do ya know what I mean? They didn't just go every Sunday and mumble 'Amen' to everything the preacher said, they were truly compassionate and Christian in the way they treated other people with kindness and respect. In a nice sort of way—it was hard to keep up."

Ellen sat atop a pile of field stones that had been scattered there near the opening of the trail into the woods, dragged from the fields by oxen, horses, and then tractors one at a time over the years, to clear for plowing. Dan leaned against a tree, concentrating on the ethereal tone of her voice as she spoke, staring into the blackness of the overgrown ravine ahead.

"So I should have trained it away, grown past it ... my defensiveness, I mean, and I did somewhat ... learned to appreciate bein' appreciated. But still sometimes the old habit of response shoots out my mouth when it's completely unwarranted."

She turned, her eyes meeting his. "That's what snapped at you today," she said. "I was angry anew at my condition, my situation ... bein' reminded of it.

"Why it is? I do not know. Why must this have been one of my definin' characteristics?

"When I would overreact like that, my husband would say, 'Delicate things must be carefully kept.' And eventually even when I reacted normally to something my husband didn't want to talk about, he would say it. His way of saying my skin was too thin.

"Delicate things must be carefully kept," she said again, and with it, Dan could see she was cradling her bundle.

"It was perhaps the one definin' negative trait I carried with me beyond my youth ... and oddly, the least necessary."

She looked down at her bundle and rocked it gently.

Dan wanted to look closely, but didn't. It felt wrong somehow, like an invasion of privacy, like staring at a woman breastfeeding a baby. He shoved his hands deep in his pockets and stepped a few steps farther into the darkness, staring into the blackness of that ravine where he had played during his youth with Tom and Ted. Several minutes passed in silence. "My turn," she finally said, looking at the tool Dan kept hooked to his belt. "Why do you wear that thing on your belt?"

Dan understood immediately that she was trying to turn the tables on his curiosity about the bundle, but he let it go. She had shared so much with him. He was again determined to reciprocate.

He placed his palm on the small tool pouch looped around his belt. The leather, worn soft as a baby's cheek from years of use was so familiar it felt like an appendage. He smiled to himself to think of how he wore it always, no matter the occasion.

"We made pistons and piston rings in the factory. Most of the jobs there could be done by just about anybody. Most folks there were just regular guys that didn't have the initiative to do anything on their own.

"I'm not looking down on 'em ... everybody's got to find what works for them. They were happy pullin' down a lever all day and a paycheck every week. But not me. I was skilled trades.

"I fixed things when they went wrong—when machines broke or got out of whack. If one of those machine operators got sick and stayed home for a week, well, they'd just put some other guy ... or gal, at the controls. But if I got sick for a week, *and I never did,*" he pointed emphatically back at her, "but if I got sick for a week, that whole place'd be in a world of hurt.

"In that place I was royalty ... with grease on my hands and calipers in my pocket ... and this all-in-one," he slapped his belt, "I was royalty. I got paid more than folks on the line and when there were layoffs, I always had a job. Us skilled tradesmen were golden.

"My dad brought me up through the ranks and taught me the ropes, got me an apprenticeship and eventually accepted me as an equal. And that meant more to me than the job. To be one of the guys with my dad, to know the pride he felt in that place, to feel like you're a part of things ... not *just* a part of things but an *important* part of things.

"But I never once acted like I was better than anybody

else there. I felt like we were a family, like the Mob or something, like we looked out for each other and took care of one another. But being a skilled tradesman, it wasn't like feeling superior gave me pride ... it was feeling like I was irreplaceable, like if I wasn't there then things wouldn't be the same, they wouldn't work right."

An idea seized him. Dan closed his eyes to the darkness and cleared his mind. He tried to form a clear image of the factory floor. He searched his memory for every shred of nuance, smell, sound, lighting that would tell Ellen what it was like to be there, to have people look to you with urgency and respect.

He struggled through it, knowing he wasn't really creating a seamless vision as she had for him. Isolated parts appeared as he was able to conjure and concentrate upon them—the view, sound, smells, the shape and workings of a grinding lathe, the heat and steam of the casting works. Looking back at the luminescent Ellen sitting there on the rocks, he could see her with her head cocked to one side, as if listening to a far-away sound.

"I see it," she said softly.

He looked back into the darkness. "And that job made me a man and the breadwinner. Even though Sue was a teller in the bank, I was the major breadwinner ... well, until she moved up to loan officer. Once she did that she was making more money than I was. That was hard to get used to, but that's okay, that's okay. I was happy for her that she found her thing. And still, on that factory floor, I was golden. So it was double good," he raised his palms to the sky.

Ellen's eyes again fell on the small, rectangular, leather pouch looped at the top through Dan's belt that hung along his right hip. It had a cover that snapped closed to conceal what was inside. The leather worn smooth and soft, the ribs at the edges gently frayed. There was a worn area on Dan's jeans beneath and just around the pouch. "So, what is that on your belt? Why do you wear it?" she asked.

Dan was taken off guard by her question—reminded how his turn had started. He looked down and then felt for it. "It's a specialized all-in-one tool. I had a toolbox on wheels, a whole load of tools, but this was what I used in a pinch.

"When you're under a machine on your back, or on your knees wedged between two lathes, that tool box is so far away."

"Can you show me?"

Dan nodded and unsnapped the cover, then easily slipped out what looked like a pair of high-tech pliers. "May I step closer?" he asked, uneasily, looking at the bundle in her lap.

She knew he was confused and curious about the bundle, the baby, but pretended not to understand his uncertainty. "Well of course you can."

Dan walked up and held the stainless steel tool out for her.

"Altogether, it's a set of pliers for gripping things." He positioned the teeth around a finger and loosely pinched the handle. "And it has a whole lot of other things inside." He spread open the handles and began pulling posts out one by one.

"There's a regular and Philips head driver, an awl, a few of the most common hex heads that fit the machines on the floor of the factory, a tiny set of calipers, a sharp knife, and ... a cork screw," he said, holding that one up with a smile, "in case you need to open a bottle of wine."

She watched his eyes, knowing he was trying not to look into the bundle, but wanting to badly. And he knew this, that it was the whole reason she'd asked him about the all-in-one.

"But ya don't use it," she said.

Still holding out the corkscrew, he pondered her tone. That had not been a question, but a statement.

"I 'spect you're right," he offered slowly, watching the expression on her face for any hints of harsh intentions, "It's mostly useless to me now."

"Then why do ya carry it if it's pointless? You don't work in the factory anymore. I don't 'magine those hex things fit anything on this old house."

Dan looked at her sadly, methodically folded up the posts, and collapsed the handles. "Habit, I guess." He slid the all-in-one back into its pouch and snapped the cover.

Her expression softened. "I'm sorry," Ellen said. "I know why ya carry it."

Dan nodded his head. "I 'spect it's for the same reason ..." his voice trailed off before diplomatically changing direction, "because it helps define who I am ... or at least who I was."

"I know," Ellen said, soothing, "I know. To set it aside would mean ... acceptance."

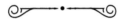

As he pulled into the driveway, the headlights swung across Kristin's face where she sat on the concrete steps before the aluminum screen door. She squinted and held a hand up to shield her eyes. Dan stepped from the truck and walked slowly toward her in the darkness.

"I thought you were asleep."

She shook her head side to side. "I was dozing ... in and out."

Dan rubbed the back of his neck and scanned the rooftops and sky beyond. He was physically and emotionally drained.

She wanted to ask where he'd been, what he'd been doing, but didn't. It didn't matter to her as much as what she had been sitting here two hours, waiting to say. After a moment of quiet she said simply, "It *is* strange being here in this place with you ... and ... I love you, too."

She had wanted to hear him open up so badly, had wanted it so long, and then had overheard it when it wasn't meant to be heard, but responded anyway as she had always dreamed of being able to do. But now, having responded, she was petrified and found she could not look at his face, so she stared across the street into the darkness.

Dan slowly milled about the gravel drive with his hands in his pockets. Finally his eyes fell on her and he knew that he must say something honest and meaningful in response. He sat beside her on the lowest step, his knees almost in his chest, and put his arm around her shoulder. She leaned back and nestled her head back into his neck and closed her eyes.

"A lot of mistakes have led me to this place," Dan offered hoarsely, "one big mistake and then a whole lot of tiny ones made over and over again. I don't really want to live here and spend my days undressing houses, but I guess I'm kinda stuck. I don't know what to do to undo it all."

"Tell Mom you love her," Kristin offered quickly. "That was the big mistake wasn't it ... letting the marriage fall apart?"

"No. The marriage fell apart because of all the little mistakes, years of little mistakes, and that can't be undone with an apology. Maybe can't be undone at all."

"Don't say that, Daddy."

Dan nestled his cheek against her hair. "Just 'cause you don't wanna hear it doesn't mean it ain't true," he said softly. "You've come here to try to help me out, to cheer me up, and maybe for me to tell you which way to go in life. I appreciate that. I love you for wanting to help me, but don't know how you can and I love you so much that I'd help you anyway I could, but you don't know what to tell you. You have to decide what you want. Concentrate on yourself and don't worry about me. I'll be alright."

"Mom still loves you, Daddy."

"Then why is she seeing another man?"

"'Cause she's lonely, I imagine." She thought of his leaving tonight—gone for a couple hours after midnight. "Have you been seeing anyone?"

Dan hesitated for a moment. "No. What living being in this world would want to see me?"

"Mom."

Dan was silent another moment. He sighed heavily. "I appreciate what you're trying to do, but it's not your job to fix these things, Sugarcube. I'm sorry, I know you want to set things right, but you can't fix this."

Kristin began to cry softly and Dan pulled her tighter.

"You made being a child so easy for me," she wept. "I never dreamed that being an adult could suck so bad. I just want to help you and Mom. It's like you're caught in some crazy world where the simplest of things, like saying 'I'm sorry,' or 'I love you,' are forbidden.

"I just want to help you Daddy."

"I know, I know," he cooed, "but some things in life cannot be undone. I can't explain it to you—have never explained it to anyone, not even myself, why it happened. Sometimes it feels as though we're all like planets, revolving around some central thing, held in place in our journey by some unseen force of nature. I once felt that way, that I was part of something bigger than myself, and that if I was pulled out it wouldn't work right anymore. Well I was pulled out of it, out of orbit I guess you'd say, only to find that it works perfectly fine without me. Somewhere in all that I lost touch with your mother."

Kristin went on crying softly, "I don't know what you're talking about Daddy. I wish I understood."

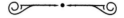

Dan and Kristin had been familiar, comfortable strangers for so long, they passed the next morning awkwardly avoiding conversation with one another, not sure of the next step in their suddenly honest relationship By eight o'clock Dan had unloaded the brackets from the back of the truck and disappeared down the street.

CHAPTER 8

It was a cool, cloudy morning. Beyond the trees, the driveway, and the road, tall corn spread out like an ocean on the gentle slope toward the river. The wind rolled across the land and the tassels and leaves bent ever so gently in unison, one row after another, and then, ignoring the man-made line, it turned across the rows, bending the tops on an unseen axis—looking like real waves on an ocean—the Indiana Ocean. Dan stood watching it, a toolbox in one hand and a cup of coffee in the other. Soon, in a year or two, maybe, this part of the ocean would all be gone, replaced by another vinyl village.

Did she sleep? Did she need to?

His eyes took in the barn, the grain house, the carriage shed, and finally the brick house, darkened scars in the eaves where the eave brackets had been. The porch gingerbread and posts were gone too, stacked now in the backyard of his apartment house. But it didn't make him sad, he figured that really, now, the house looked more like it did when Ellen was alive, before it was done over in the Italianate style for her husband's second wife. Though it didn't trigger sadness, he could sense *that* emotion on the horizon, that deconstructing this house could become painful.

Dan opened the front door and went upstairs, taking in the dank atmosphere of the house in slow measured steps. He opened his toolbox and got to work cleaning a hundred years of paint from the slot of the hinge screws on a door in the northeast bedroom. Once he had the door off and laid out on the floor, he methodically went about removing the hinges, the rim lock, knobs, knob collar, and escutcheon. It took an hour to pull all the room's woodwork loose.

He knelt on the floor to organize the dismantled pieces when, from some distant corner of the house, came that lonely, beckoning whistle. Four forlorn notes echoed along the plastered walls and wood plank floors. Dan cocked his head to one side and tried to locate the sound. It died away. She was here, somewhere, he knew it. He could feel the tingling edge of expectation setting the hair on the back on his neck up straight, but went on working.

"My babies were all born in this room," her voice came from behind him, "and this is where I died."

Dan turned to see Ellen standing in the bare doorway, looking down at the door and the scattered pieces of hardware and woodwork spread out on the floor.

"Eighteen months after James was born I had a third child, another boy, Jack. Jack was *my* gift from God. You never say it to 'em, never even admit to yerself that ya favor one over another, but I loved my little Jack so much I can feel it still."

Dan smiled up at her, then felt it come to him again as he knelt there on the floor, a sensation that overtook his vision and hearing, in fact all his senses, as if he were no longer in this world. Color and light burst into his mind like fireworks against a darkened sky, the sparkling blast eventually overtaking the black. The sun was suddenly terribly bright, the air that met his nostrils, at once dry. He was moving along a dirt road; the Ballard farmhouse was ahead to the left. Red and yellow leaves scattered across the road and cotton puffs of clouds punctuated a deep blue sky. To the right of his view a bare-chested, barefoot boy skipped along in cut-off pants, a cotton glove and a length of twine in his hand. As they moved along the boy chirped questions, hopped on one foot, looking up enthusiastically, like an eager puppy begging to play.

"When will the baby come, Mama?"

"Any day now," Dan heard Ellen's voice come out of him. But he was her, traveling in her form.

"Will it be a boy or a girl?"

"Only God knows."

"When will God send it?"

Dan felt a smile spread wide across his face. "Any day now," Ellen's voice eased out of him.

In this purely defined vision Dan followed the child down a grassy path toward the river, beneath a sheltering grove of trees. Leaves overhead blew loose and spun in the air before rolling west in a barren, recently plowed field. He was seeing things from Ellen's perspective; he knew it, seeing a moment from a warm day in the autumn a century and a half before.

But this was the third time she had drawn Dan into a memory and as intoxicating as it was, he was seeing more, exploring the moment. The contrast of colors and tones in the leaves and bark, blades of grass and plowed up earth, it was too much, slightly unnatural. At the edge of the field a milkweed plant was strangled by a wild morning glory vine. The trumpet-shaped flowers—deep purple fading into pale violet, were crayon box colors: too pure, too intense to be natural. The sky was bluer than any blue Dan had ever seen; the green of the grasses was almost luminous. The brown, red, and yellow of the changing leaves were richer and more velvety than the thick liquid beneath the lid of a freshly mixed gallon of paint. This wasn't just a motion picture memory from her life, but a re-creation, built piece by piece.

The brown-haired boy ran ahead, mischievously disappearing into a solid line of trees. He heard Ellen's voice call out from within him, "Slow down, honey, Mama can't go so fast." The child giggled and ran on.

With that Dan looked further into the scene, feeling, and knowing now that Ellen was pregnant. The weight was there, shoulders were forced back to compensate, there was tightness in the hips, making each plodding step a chore. As the path neared a tightening cluster of trees the shoulder of the boy came into view behind a towering walnut. There was a pretending not to see. Splatters of silver and green reflected off the river between the tree trunks ahead as he passed into the woods. The boy sprung out from behind the tree and shouted "Boo!" and then ran on down the path toward the river.

The scene was bathed in soothing contentment; all was right with the world. Dan didn't want it to end. His own chest swelled with emotion as he gave himself over to the vision and her emotions, feeling what she had felt, seeing what she saw, following the child on down the matted path to the river.

Jack hurried to the water's edge. "Stay in the shallows," Dan heard Ellen's voice call out of him again as he sat on a large rock beside the water. Jack slipped the glove onto his right hand.

Before them ran a dark, thirty-foot-wide section of river between the bank and a tiny eyebrow of an island. Beyond the island the body of the shallow river passed slowly. Water ran smooth over four-foot-deep trenches and rippled over pebble-strewn shallows, swirling gently over swaying water grasses reaching toward the muddy banks. The covered bridge, sitting on stone slab pillars that rose thirty feet out of the water, shadowed a wide swath of the river.

Jack hurried into the water and waded to a small piece of rope tied to a sapling at the bank, the other end of rope rose out of the water at the island, tied to another small tree. He lifted the trout line and shrieked when up came a fat, black catfish hanging from a hook on the first line.

Jack's large, lively brown eyes darted over his shoulder, his round cherubic face beaming broadly, "Got one." He gripped the fish with the gloved hand and worked the hook loose from its mouth, then carefully tied it on the extra piece of twine.

Beyond the thin island a large flock of geese swooped down below the trees as if entering a tunnel and lighted in the river in long, dragging splashes. Jack went on checking each line and found two more, smaller catfish. "Aw, they're not as big, Mama."

"They'll still taste good."

"Yup, they sure will."

As he worked fastidiously to loosen a hook from the shining, black fish, he ran the tip of his tongue along his upper lip.

Up he pulled the remaining lines and hooks. "The little

ones have stolen all the rest of my worms." He was up to his waist in the water, his small, tanned, muscular body reflected in the water. "Aw, Mama. Worms! I forgot to bring the worms. Dang!" he said, "I can't reset the hooks."

Quickly the fishing was forgotten. The catfish were tied to a tree and Jack leapt into the larger body of the river, scattering geese to the sky as he jumped and yelled. He climbed on the fallen trunk of a tree trapped in a sandy shallow and stood upright, the sun glimmering off his wet skin. He held his hands out, palms to the sky, and fell backward like a stiff board into a deeper patch of water.

The boy went on in reckless abandon, splashing in the water and then standing on a sandbar, flinging rock after rock at the long covered bridge that hung high in the air, each one making a dull thud as they bounced off the whitewashed siding. All the while, the eyes Dan had been loaned, followed with delight.

Finally a whistle called out from within him, the same four notes, starting with two beats of the same note, sliding up to the third and then falling to the fourth.

"Aw Mama," Jack moaned from across the river.

"Come now," she called out.

As they made their way up the bank, toward the lane to the house, the vision slowly faded and Dan found himself right there on the floor, sitting back on his heels as he had been when the vision started. He struggled for awareness.

"Can you imagine a hundred and fifty years of replaying those memories?" she asked sadly. She turned her back and stared out the window. "I'm tired, Dan, tired in a way that's hard to explain."

Ellen seemed to shake herself back to some previously intended point. "Some women have their babies in bunches, but conceiving was never easy for me, so there were gaps of several years between Beaul and James and then between Jack and ... my last child," her voice trailed off.

Dan watched her talk for a moment, and then tried to get back to his work, but it was hard, feeling like he'd just woken from a long sleep.

"My last child didn't really make it into this world, did not ever take a breath of fresh air before leavin' this world, caught up in the physical me and then the spiritual me."

She sat on the front edge of the windowsill telling her story, her eyes following him about the room, watching him arrange its doors, woodwork, and floor grates.

"It was the night of that very day, the one you just saw. That was my last day, the last day I could have any effect over my world. I went into labor just before dinner. The doctor did make it. And I struggled, oh, how I struggled—but nothing, no progress. He worked at me and tried to reassure me. The pressure was maddening. Finally I was so tired that I just closed my eyes, hopin' to doze. I think he thought I'd fallen unconscious. He stood and backed away and said, 'It's in God's hands now.'

"And it was."

Dan sat back, resting against the wall, watching her as she spoke.

"My mother-in-law let out a terrible cry.

"'Breech,' the doctor said simply, and my mother-in-law began sobbing, one arm wrapped tightly around my head and the other hand gripping mine tightly. I began to cry, too."

She purposefully stopped speaking and stared squarely at Dan, sitting against the wall. "Close yer eyes ... and hold on."

Immediately Dan's vision went dark and then came back to him, lit only by coal oil lamps on the dresser and bedside stand. The room had been transformed. He was not within her, seeing things from her perspective, but on the floor, sitting in the exact same position he'd been in a moment earlier. She had taken him there to that moment, to her death.

Ellen lay in the bed, pale, her hair drenched from sweat. Dan knew immediately that the man standing was the doctor. Another man and an older woman knelt by the bed, Ellen's husband and mother-in-law. Their shadows flickered on the walls.

"I want to talk to them," Ellen cried through clenched teeth. "This may be my last chance. Please!"

Her husband staggered from the room, weeping, wiping at his nose and eyes with a wrist. Ellen lay moaning. The woman knelt beside her and pressed a damp cloth on her forehead. A moment later, three children stepped cautiously into the room with their father, looks of fear on their faces. They were lined up beside the bed. The oldest, a dark haired girl in her early teens, was weeping.

"Now I want you children to be good," she struggled to say. "You remember the things I've taught you."

The young girl fell to her knees and sobbed into the pillow beside her mother's face. As a wave of pain hit Ellen, her eyes rolled halfway back, her eyelids fluttered, and she let out a harrowing scream that sent a shudder through the children. The smallest, Jack, winced, steeling himself against the horrible sound. She forced her mind back to them.

"Beaul, I'm countin' on you to help your grandmother."

Beaul shook her head, a look of terror on her face. "Please don't die, Mama," she wept.

The vision was so real. Dan could feel the bound edge of the carpet under the palms of his hand and a breeze from the open window cooled the back of his neck. The smells, the flicker of firelight, the sounds of voices were so immediate that he almost lost recognition that this was an event long past. He ached for her impending loss along with her family. He fought the urge to kneel beside the bed with them. In desperation he shouted at the doctor, "You primitive fool, do something!" There was no recognition from any of them that he'd made any sound and he knew he was an observer, it was all past, all unfixable. He began to cry with them.

The older boy, James, standing behind Beaul, showed no emotion, frozen in the moment, but the small boy, Jack, seemed suddenly to understand what was happening. His face crumbled. "No!" he shrieked. He pushed ahead of his brother and sister and hugged his mother.

"No, you can't die, Mama! I won't let you go, I won't let you leave," he cried. His father bent to pull him away, but Jack held fast.

"No!" he cried again in anguish, "If we hold her tight she won't be able to go, she'll have to stay right here!"

"It don't work that way," his father said, grabbing Jack's arm and pulling him off Ellen. He took the boy by the shoulders and looked into his face. Jack looked back at his mother, searching, tears streaming down his cheeks.

"Now look, Jack," his father started.

"No, Daddy!" the boy pleaded. "God was suppose to send a baby. Mama said so. Will the baby still come? Who will take care of it if Mama goes away?" He tore loose and scrambled onto the bed, wrapping his arms around Ellen's neck again. "Don't go, Mama!" Her head fell limp to one side.

Dan pulled himself out. In desperation he cleared his mind of the moment and forced his mind back. He was out of breath. Ellen was standing across the room, staring back at him. He raised his arm and wiped his tears with a shirtsleeve. He scanned the room, comparing the now tattered bright space with the darkened room he'd just left.

Ellen turned away and paced the floor. "I don't know why I didn't just go with it. There are times when the inevitable is so big and obvious, you got to just accept it to really survive. But I didn't. After I passed on there was a moment of absolute calm and peace, like nothin' you could ever imagine. For a moment I was floatin' above 'em, out of myself, lookin' down on Jack holdin' on to my body. Somethin' was pullin' me away. But I held on to that other little soul and fought against the obvious and against the pull, too, clingin' to the earth and the house and my family. And that's what's trapped me here. I suppose I could leave, just walk on beyond the edge of the property and come apart, but I haven't been able to bring myself to do it, even though there's nothin' holdin' me back."

There was a moment of silence. Dan stared blankly into the scattered pieces of hardware. Neither of them said anything for several minutes.

"I don't have anything to offer you in return," Dan finally said softly, an admission of failure.

She looked back at him, "What do you mean?"

"I can't create dreams like ... pictures of my life that you could step into."

Ellen smiled sympathetically, "I got no complaints, Dan. The tit-for-tat, that was never about me getting something specific from you. Sometimes the best thing a friend can do is listen."

The thought was nice, but it didn't satisfy Dan. He knew he could never give her back anything near what she had shared with him. Not knowing what to say, he silently turned back toward his work.

He pulled a handful of large, zip-lock plastic bags from his toolbox and began to organize rim locks, hinges, window locks and pulls in several piles. Ellen knelt before him and watched as he filled a bag with window locks.

"Why are these things worth money?" she asked, forcing the subject away. "I see all the clever things modern people have and use and I can't imagine that these things have any value."

"There are people with houses like this who are trying to restore 'em. They need these old things to put their houses back in order, to fix things."

"Where are they sold?"

"At special antique stores called salvage yards."

"Special? I don't understand."

Dan scooped up the random screws scattered about the floor and dropped them into a bag. "Most antique stores are filled with old furniture and toys, hundred-year-old dishes and oil lamps. Anything you used during your life can be found in an antique store. The older the better. The kitchenware you used, the toys your children played with, the tools your husband used: all antiques worth money. The finer the condition, the better. But there are only a few stores in the central part of the state that specialize in old house parts, catering to people who are restoring old houses. That's where all this stuff will go."

"How did you figure out that you could make money this way?"

"My truck broke down in front of one of these antique salvage yards a couple years back. While I waited for a tow I went in and got to looking at all that old stuff. Few days later I saw an old house being torn down and all the good things that were worth money were being destroyed. Most people tearing down houses don't know that this stuff is worth money. They just think it's old junk. So I found a little niche I could fill."

Ellen started to speak, but interrupted herself with a gasp. Suddenly her eyes spread wide and her mouth dropped open. "Oh ma-gosh, I can't believe I didn't notice ..." She stood and backed through the wall, disappearing beneath the plaster surface.

"D-a-d-d-y," a singsong voice called out from below.

Dan was confused. His mind was still in the conversation, only to be jolted by the sound of Kristin's voice.

"D-a-d-d-y," she sung out again.

In a moment she appeared at the top of the stairs, clad in jeans and a white, V-neck T-shirt, tucking her blonde hair behind her ears. She smiled broadly and stepped gingerly into the dirty space. "Well there you are, and with your bags of goodies."

"Hey, Sugarcube," Dan said nervously, uncertain about having Kristin here in Ellen's house.

"What do you have here?" she asked. "Anything worth-while?"

"Woodwork and hardware," Dan said simply, gathering up the bags and nodding toward an empty Gordon's Gin box he'd pulled from the liquor store dumpster that morning. She handed him the box and knelt in front of him, helping place the bags inside.

"What brings you here?" he asked.

"I'd like to help you," she said with an urgent sputter, in the same pleading way she'd asked for ice cream as a child, fearing he'd say no. "I could come here with you and help you take things apart and clean them up. Is there much more to do?"

Dan smiled and shook his head dismissively, "Aw, that's a nice thought, but you don't want to do this dirty work.

There's the rest of the doors and hardware and woodwork to remove, the staircase and heat vents." He went on filling the cardboard box.

"Please Daddy," Kristin said, reaching out and touching his sleeve to get him to stop and really consider it, "I want to help you, I want to help you in some meaningful way and I don't know how else to do it."

Dan didn't want to say yes, didn't want to ruin this time with Ellen, but he loved Kristin so and found it hard to disappoint her. How could he say no without hurting her? And he considered for a moment that this might be a way for him to reciprocate, to show Ellen *his* gift from God.

"Well, that would be nice," he finally replied. "Thank you." As he begrudgingly relented he was filled with a sense of understanding from Ellen. She approved of this arrangement, of having Dan's daughter here each day. Wherever she was, however she located herself here, she was listening and communicating with him, again, without words, but with pure, seamless, understanding.

Kristin helped Dan pull out the closet doors and strip them of their hardware and organize the pieces in appropriate bags. She watched carefully as he showed her how to clean paint from the surface of a screw with an old chisel and run the point of an awl down the groove until enough paint was out to turn the screw with a fine-point screwdriver. They talked throughout the afternoon and Dan, having grown used to solitary work, was reminded of the comfort of workplace camaraderie. She was easy company.

CHAPTER 9

Near 5 o'clock they loaded the doors and hardware in the truck. Dan pulled a can of Coke from his cooler and shared it with Kristin as they sat on the tailgate looking up at the house. He remembered Ellen looking out at him from the upstairs window on that first terrifying day and wondered what she thought of Kristin. She had been about, somehow, somewhere, all afternoon; he'd felt it. And he knew now she was observing.

"Is your Mom put-out that you're staying with me?" Dan asked, passing Kristin the Coke.

This uncharacteristic directness caught her off guard. "She doesn't mind. We talked about it. She thought it would be a good idea."

Dan raised an eyebrow. "Thought it would be a good idea?"

"Yeah. I'm surprised you're surprised. Mom cares about you. She's worried about how you're doing."

"So she put you up to this."

"No, don't think that," Kristin said quickly, reaching out and rubbing his shoulder. "I mentioned it to Mom first and asked if it would hurt her feelings if I didn't stay with her this summer."

"Why didn't you call and ask me before you came?" Dan snorted.

"I was afraid you'd say no," she said. "Sometimes it's easier to ask forgiveness than to ask permission."

Dan nodded and smiled wide, continuing to look up at the house. He put his hand out and rubbed her shoulder in return. "I 'spect you're right."

They sat in silence, each taking ever smaller drinks from the can before passing it back, neither wanting to finish it.

"Imagine the lawn needs mowing over at your Mom's," he mumbled, wiping the back of his neck with a handkerchief.

"You mow, I'll trim," she said.

"Alright then."

Sue was not home. They let themselves into the garage and got to work. Dan mowed and Kristin followed behind with the trimmer. When they were done Dan got two beers out of the garage refrigerator and sat gulping his on the front steps while Kristin swept the sidewalk.

"Whatd'ya know about this fella your Mom's been seein'?" Dan asked.

Kristin swept a moment before answering, unaccustomed to this change in her normally nonverbal father. "Well, he's a manager of some sort with the bank. Seems like a nice man."

It was a hurtful subject, but Dan couldn't help himself from prying more. "Must make a lot of money."

This was a topic still tender for her, too. She kept sweeping without looking at him. "Well, he's got a big house on the lake, so he must be doing alright."

"You've met him?"

"Yeah. His name is Frank Wilson."

Dan tipped the beer up, then wiped his mouth with the back of his hand. "Does it bother you for your mother to be seein' somebody?"

She stopped sweeping and looked at him, sitting there on the same front step where he'd sat and watched her ride her first new bike, where he stood with her mother waving goodbye as she left for her first prom and again for her first year at IU. "Yes, it bothers me," she said, her jaw tight and trembling, tears welling up in her eyes. "Does it bother you?"

Dan's expression remained impassive. He didn't want to answer, didn't want to admit to her how he felt. He tipped his head and shrugged his shoulders before standing and moving toward the mower.

His seeming indifference, his quick return to silence angered her. He'd drawn her out on an emotional limb and then left her there alone. She took a couple steps toward him dragging the broom behind her, "I can't make you talk if you don't want to, but don't ask me about my feelings if you're not gonna to share yours with me."

"I'm sorry I brought it up," Dan said, starting to push the mower toward the garage.

"Daddy," she went on, tears trickling down her cheeks, following half-heartedly behind him, "don't think for a minute that she's doing this to make you jealous! She's not. She's doing it trying not to think of you at all! She's doing it for herself!

She's lonely."

Dan went on, disappearing around the side of the garage.

Kristin stood in the driveway leaning against the broom handle, wiping her eyes with the back of her hand.

Her mother's car came down 16th and pulled into the drive, followed by a Cadillac.

"You okay?" her mother said, stepping out of the car.

"Just something stuck in my eye," Kristin said.

Frank Wilson stepped out of his car smiling broadly, "Hello Kristin, nice to see you again."

He was tall and slender, several years older than her mother, white hair and a dark tan, looking like he'd just stepped off a golf course. Kristin shook his hand and managed a smile.

Dan came around the garage wiping his hands on a paper towel. Awkward, polite eyes, masking social terror, met his. Only Frank Wilson was poised in the moment.

"Well, we're all here," Sue sighed, wringing her hands. She plunged ahead, "Dan, I'd like you to meet Frank ... this is Frank Wilson."

Dan came forward, his face stiffened, his composure measured. As he shook Frank's hand, for Dan, Sue, and Kristin, the moment hung for an eternity, each of them feeling that in the ways they defined themselves upon each other, the earth had shifted. Each of the three, perhaps more clearly than any of them wanted, saw their interpersonal landscape for what it now was. Sue wasn't a wife, but an ex-wife. Kristin wasn't just a daughter, but a potential step-daughter. And Sue saw Dan, her high school sweetheart and husband of twenty-six years as an outsider—an outsider in her life, in appearance, in the landscape of the town that had once been theirs, even on the lawn he had earned and tended half his life.

"Well," Dan added quickly, breaking the spell of realization, "I 'spect we're done here. Put the broom away," he said to Kristin, "and we'll be on our way. Pleased to meet you Frank."

"Yes, pleasure to meet you," Frank said.

With that, Kristin, shell shocked, did as her father suggested. Like him, she wanted to get as far away from the moment as possible.

Once in the truck, she silently started to cry. "I'm sorry I pressed you, Daddy," she moaned, tears trickling down her cheeks. "Of course it bothers you. I didn't have to ask."

Dan pulled away from the curb and from the rearview mirror watched Sue and Frank walk into the house, the home he'd worked so many years to buy, so many years to care for. So much was not his anymore. "It's okay," he said, "sometimes, maybe, you have to hear something ... and see it, to really feel it."

After a morning spent stripping woodwork and doors from the upstairs, they sat on the tailgate beneath the shade of a maple and ate fast food. Dan picked at french fries, dipping bits into a pool of ketchup on the wax paper wrapper. He watched the yellow and black spinning bowl of a cement truck off in the distance as it poured the foundation for a model home.

Kristin watched him watching the construction crews. Since the night he came home late and opened up a little to her they hadn't had the real heart to heart she hoped would grow out of that fitful start. He seemed different since that night, more relaxed, more ready to offer an opinion or share a personal insight. He'd clammed up yesterday before meeting Frank, but later gave her another opening. She wanted to pry him farther open, to get him to talk openly about his marriage to her mother. If he could do it with her, maybe he could do it with her mother.

Kristin tried to choose her words carefully, but they came out awkward anyway. "If you don't want to talk about it, you know, if it's too personal, I'd understand, but you said the other night, when you came home late, that some things can't be undone between you and Mom. What things? What happened between you and Mom that was so bad it can't be undone?"

Dan gave a mildly exasperated smile to the grass and grumbled with his mouth full, "You just don't give up, do ya?"

Kristin didn't reply. She didn't want to apologize or soothe in any way that would let him off the hook. It was futile, she figured, but she couldn't help but ask. He swallowed his mouthful and astonished her by actually replying.

"It's a funny thing about most of life's problems, people want to be told that the solution is one thing," he said, raising one finger. He turned to her, "But it's almost never just one thing."

She held a chicken sandwich between her hands, took a bite, and looked away, now suddenly unnerved that her father might actually serve up what she had wanted so desperately to know.

"I mean, gun crime," he continued, "abortion, drug abuse ... it's never just one thing that causes it, is it? You couldn't change just one thing and fix any of those problems. Well, personal problems are that way too."

Dan took another bite of his sandwich and readjusted himself on the tailgate. "It was a little bit you and your brother I guess ... and life ... growing older ... being parents and spouses and breadwinners instead of young lovers. We built our world around you two kids. The focus was never on your mother and me, it was always on giving you the absolute best opportunity."

He thought better about what he'd just said and uncharacteristically reached out and patted her sleeve. "I'm not blamin' you. Your mother and I chose that way to live ... or more rightly, fell into it ... out of our love for you and your brother and feelings of responsibility, and hell, all the other parents were doing it. But after years of changing diapers and organizing your life around little league baseball and soccer practice and games, school open houses, workin' overtime to pay for things and savin' for the future ... your kids can go off to school and you look at your husband or wife and say, 'what happened to us? Where did that young, fun person go? Who's this middle-aged stranger I'm livin' with?' Your mom and me just never put our marriage first. Somewhere along the way we stopped being the focus of the marriage and you and your brother took over ... in our minds, mind you. I'm not saying you did this. Your mother and me did.

"And you know me, I don't know how to talk about these things very well, I wasn't raised to be all self-confessional all the time. I mean, life ain't Dr. Phil. I didn't know how to say, 'Sue, we need to set aside time for us?'" he gestured with two open palms, as if the time would fit in the space between his hands.

"I didn't even know that was a problem until we'd already forgot how to spend time together. And that silence, that not talkin' about things is like building a little wall. The less you talk the bigger the wall gets. I guess that's what people mean when they say they grew apart."

Dan took another bite of his sandwich and washed it down with a swig of Coke. "There's one, okay?" he said holding up a finger again. "That's the first part of it."

"And wait," he said abruptly, "you promise me something. When you have kids, you put your marriage first in the day-to-day living you do. If you don't have a strong marriage then you don't really have much to offer your kids beyond physical comfort. The marriage should come first and the children revolve around it ... in general ... not the marriage revolving around the kids the way most people do it today. Promise?"

"Promise," she answered before taking a drink, still avoiding his eyes.

Dan forgot that there were other points on his list and stared out beyond the sheltering canopy of trees at the far-off cement truck driver hosing out his equipment.

"Building that wall is a process, a process of steps ... neglecting affection for days and weeks and months and years, missed opportunities, the ... things ... that aren't shared when your attention is constantly trained on survival and parenting ... these become habits ... deeply ingrained habits of behavior. So when you add up all those missed opportunities to show love, all those hours of silence ... interacting between two people ... Hell, I am on Dr. Phil, now," he chuckled, shaking his head and easing himself off the tailgate.

"Anyway," he went on searching for words, "how do you undo all that, all those years of acting that way? It just seems like a one-way journey and I don't think you can retrace your steps. And when you two kids were finally both gone at college, well there it was; the distance between us was just laid bare. There wasn't this focus of our lives that held us together anymore, there was just ... silence. Before you kids came along we were ... a young couple, we were ...

lovers, but by the time you kids were gone we were just ... mutual parents without kids. It's like we didn't know how to get back to that place where we had a real relationship ... at least I didn't know how."

Dan paced silently about in the dry grass with his hands in his pockets. In one respect there was something nourishing and cleansing about saying these things to Kristin, knowing full well that he was also saying them to Ellen, that she was hearing as well. In another respect there was the old Dan feeling revealed and pathetic, like some crybaby moaning about his problems.

Kristin spoke up meekly, "Didn't Mom try to fix things?"

"Yeah," Dan admitted sharply, nodding his head, "but whether I was too proud or just plain bullheaded ... ya know ... about saying how I felt, I couldn't do it. I couldn't go to counseling and cry about things with some stranger."

"And you couldn't do it with your wife either," she said.

He paced the worn ground again, "Nope. Guess not."

They passed an awkward silence. Finally he laughed to himself, imagining what she was thinking.

"It sounds really pathetic and stupid when it's all said out in the open like this. To at least have a chance to save it, all I had to do was admit that we had a problem and go to counseling with her ... swallow my pride. But I couldn't do it."

"Too strong," Kristin put in for him.

"No, Sugarcube. Too weak, I think, now."

"How so?"

He sat back down on the tailgate, grimacing. "Men think they're being strong when they hold it all inside. But that's not right, is it? Women are superior to men that way."

"I'm surprised to hear you say that."

"It's true. I didn't know it then, when we divorced. But I know it now. If a man was strong he wouldn't be afraid to cry, afraid to say how he feels. Holding it in is the true sign of weakness."

He rubbed the back of his sun-reddened neck with a weathered hand, then started gathering up the fast food wrappers. "I watched you being born, I was there. Any man who can watch a woman give birth to a baby and then still think he's stronger because his muscles are bigger and he doesn't cry, is a fuckin' fool. And ... I've been a fuckin' fool many times."

Kristin knew there were more points to the story of the divorce and her father's current predicament, but she would not go for the slam dunk, would not push him any further. He had said more than she ever dreamed he would. And anyway, she needed time to digest it herself.

"I love you, Daddy," she said, wanting to reassure him that it was okay to be so honest. "I'm glad that you're my father."

"I love you too, Sugarcube," he said looking at her, a McDonalds bag in his hand. He patted her knee, "We're okay, aren't we?"

"Yep, we're okay."

They gathered up the last of the trash about the tailgate in silence. As Kristin tossed the wadded-up bags toward the front of the bed of the truck Dan posed a question that puzzled her:

"Do you believe in ... spirits?"

She turned and gave him a quizzical smile. "You mean ghosts?"

He shrugged his shoulders and nodded, "Yeah, spirits, ghosts ... whatever you want to call 'em."

"I don't know," she laughed, "not really." She studied his expression. "Why? Do you?"

"Well, I see things and hear things in these old houses when I'm all alone. Indistinct, far-off voices that turn out to be ... oh ... I don't know ... wind in the trees. Sometimes I see things move at the edges of my peripheral vision, but when I turn to look directly, there's nothin' there. That sort of thing."

"Here?" she asked.

He was testing her, just in case Ellen made an appearance. How much was just enough to plant the seed of possibility in her without revealing anything material?

"I know it sounds crazy," he laughed uncertainly, "but the first day I was here, in the barn, up in the loft, I was certain that somethin' was comin' at me, but just disappeared into thin air. Call me crazy if you want."

"No!" Kristin scowled. "You're serious?"

"Was probly nothing," he said, waving his hand in the air dismissively before turning and walking toward the house. "Still, makes ya wonder, don't it?"

She followed him, "Now you've given me the willies."

He stopped and turned toward her. "What would you do if you saw a spirit?"

"I'd shit my pants," she laughed.

"Yeah, me too," he smiled, moving back toward the house.

From behind them a lumbering Chevy Suburban turned into the driveway, kicking up dust as it left the gravel and pulled into the grass near them. A petite, neatly dressed woman climbed down out of the driver's seat and smiled broadly at them. She looked as though she'd just stepped out of a corporate boardroom. Her shoulder length brown hair was held in place by a thick layer of hair spray, looking as much like a helmet as real hair. She wore a black blazer and slacks with a blue blouse.

"Are ya'll the people doin' salvage work here?" she called in a sharp, high-pitched tone. "Are you the salvage man?"

Dan nodded and walked toward her.

"I want that barn," she shot rapidly in a clear, southern, Paula Deen accent. "Hi, I'm Mary Beth Ward." She thrust out her hand and smiled a huge insincere smile, "and I was wantin' that barn and I tracked down this fella? ... Tom?"

"Yeah," Dan cut in, "Dan Reynolds ... my daughter Kristin," he nodded toward her. "You must have met Tom ..."

"Yeah," she interrupted, "pleasure to meet ya. Well anyway, that developer said that I should talk to you, that you had salvage rights. So I'm here to make a deal, Mr. Salvage Man. I want that barn!"

Dan smiled incredulous. "Call me Dan. What do you mean you want the barn?"

"Well ..." Ignoring Dan, she tucked her purse under her arm and marched clumsily toward the barn, the spikes of her high heals sinking into the dirt with each step. She kicked off her shoes and gripped them between two fingers and a thumb, then walked on, barefoot, calling over her shoulder, "I'm opening a restaurant downtown in the old Woolworth's building and I want the interior decor to look like the inside of a barn."

Dan and Kristin followed. Dan whispered over his shoulder, "Too much makeup."

Kristin whispered back, smiling and raising her eyebrows, "Too much hair."

The woman didn't hear a thing, but went on, stopping at the opening of the barn doors.

"You see, what I wanna do ..." she waited for the two to catch up. "What I wanna do on the interior of my main dining room is cover the walls with barn siding, then attach the beams to that so it looks like you're inside a barn," she gushed. "I'm gonna call it 'The Loft.' Get it?"

"Yeah, I get it," Dan said slowly.

Kristin spoke up, "The old Woolworth's store is a really neat building, especially on the inside, tin ceilings and everything."

"Oh, but I don't want that gaudy Victorian thing. I want it to look more rustic. So, what do you say, Mr. Reynolds? Will you sell me the barn?"

Dan shrugged his shoulders and raised both eyebrows, "Well, sure, but takin' this thing apart ain't gonna be easy."

"How much?" Mary Beth shot quickly. "Now, I'll need you to take it apart and just stack it up here for my contractor—one pile of barn siding and another pile of beams. He'll come load it all up when you're done."

"Well, I don't know," Dan stammered.

"Two thousand bucks?"

"You down there working at that building most days?" Dan asked. "Cause I'd need to think this through and then stop by and give you a price."

"Well, sure," she blurted with a smile so big and forced it looked like it might break her face in half. "Just stop by later today or tomorrow and we'll work something out."

Outside the barn's huge open sliding door rain fell in relentless sheets in the darkness. Ellen stood near a feeding stall and watched Dan watch the rain.

"Why do ya do it," she asked? "Why do ya strip houses? There must have been other options for you, with your skills, there must have been other ways to make a livin'."

Dan didn't answer, but shifted from one foot to the other, hands in his pockets, staring out at the downpour.

"I ask," she went on, "'cause, though you appear to be good at it, I sense that it bothers you, that you don't really like doin' it."

"After I lost my job, I was lost," Dan said. "Every job I saw just looked so demeaning. I'd go from being indispensable to being just another worker—and for half the money I'd been making before. That was hard to take. And so I didn't work for more than a year. That was a big mistake. I was livin' off unemployment and Sue's paycheck, which drove me farther into ... well, I just lost my self-respect. As we got closer and closer to the divorce, I started looking for something I could do independently.

"I guess all this talking to you and Kristin has made me admit to myself that I wanted to work alone because I was ashamed of my situation and I didn't want anybody else to know how pathetic I'd become."

There was a long silence. The rain clattered on the corrugated roof of the barn.

"Looks like yer gonna sell the pieces of this barn."

"Somehow," Dan looked up at the timbers overhead, "I've got to figure out how to take it apart quickly and cheaply without the whole thing falling in on me and Kristin in the process."

"How long 'till there's nothing left of this place?" she asked cautiously, half-afraid to hear the answer.

Dan looked at her, searching the meaning, the meaning of her perhaps having no place else to exist. "Couple weeks, at the outside, maybe."

Another awkward silence.

"Where will you go? What will you do?" he asked.

Ellen shrugged her shoulders, "I don't know. I can't imagine being here with it all gone."

Dan stepped toward her. "There's gonna be a retention pond right here," he said, pointing to the ground with both hands, thinking she wasn't taking it seriously enough, "maybe fifteen feet deep in the center, right here and thirty yards across. They're gonna wipe this place clean. You'll never know it was here."

"I'll know."

"I mean nobody *living* will know."

"You'll know."

"Hell, I'm as invisible as you are," Dan sighed, shaking his head.

She tried to stare him down but it didn't work.

"Ellen," he insisted, "your ..." he gestured wide with his hands up toward the barn beams, "whole structure is going to come down. There won't be anything left. I don't know what you need to survive, but if you need this farm to have any physical or spiritual similarity to what you knew to survive, you're going to be in a world of hurt. You'll have the graveyard ... they'll have to save that."

"Melodramatic," she snorted.

"Regardless, it will be all you're left with."

CHAPTER 10

The upstairs rooms had been stripped bare. The raised, four panel doors were stacked deep in the old kitchen. Dan and Kristin had filled a cardboard box with rim locks and window locks and cast iron hinges. The nails had been pulled from the backside of the trim and baseboard, all now stacked neatly on the kitchen floor. They spent the better part of the morning dismantling the walnut stair rail that had gracefully bent at the landings, the balustrade and the turned newel post at the base of the steps, its intricate and delicate rounded top worn smooth from generations of hands rubbing it as they met the stairs. Just before noon, as they were beginning to remove the doors from the downstairs rooms, Sue's car pulled into the drive.

"It's Mom," Kristin said, peering out an east side window. A few moments later Sue appeared in the front door with a pizza box in her hands. She stepped gingerly through the dirty front hall and sitting room in high heels and a skirt.

"Anybody hungry?" she called into the old house.

Kristin and Sue sat on the tailgate of the truck and Dan settled on the cooler in the grass before them. The three shared polite conversation while they ate.

Kristin's iPhone vibrated on the metal tailgate. She squinted down at the number, then impulsively pinched the silence button, drawing her hand back quickly as if she'd touched a hot stove. Her eyes focused apprehensively upon it as it vibrated several more times, making a dull metallic hum on the tailgate, until it mercifully went to voice mail.

Kristin absentmindedly went back to her piece of pizza. Dan raised an eyebrow and exchanged a searching glance with Sue.

Kristin looked up. "What?" she said, meeting first her mother's, then father's gaze. After taking in their bemused expressions she begrudgingly offered an exasperated, "Lilly."

"Lilly?" Sue asked. "You sent them a resume?"

Dan smiled broadly at his daughter, but she showed no emotion. She swung her head to one side, flinging the blonde hair out of her face, avoiding eye contact. She tipped a can to her mouth and drank, then went on eating.

"Why didn't you answer it?" Dan smiled, incredulous. Moments went by without an answer.

His smile faded, eyes squinting in examination. "You're afraid."

Though Kristin was unmoved, Sue was taken aback by Dan's accusation. She watched him testing their daughter.

Kristin shrugged again and swallowed a mouthful of pizza. "Why would I be afraid of a phone call? It's just that

... I'm eating. I don't want to stop and talk while I'm eating. I'll call 'em back."

Her cell phone chimed and simultaneously buzzed once, drawing each eye and triggering another moment of heavy silence between them.

"Because with opportunity comes obligation," Dan continued. "There might be a choice in that voice mail, a choice you might not be ready to make."

"I'm not afraid of anything," she said in frustration. She tossed a piece of crust into the pizza box, grabbed the phone, pressed the screen several times, and then held it to her ear listening intently. She eventually set it back down on the tailgate and without a word picked up another slice of pizza.

Dan, exasperated, spread his hands wide, "Gimme a fuckin' break. What did they say?"

"Let me guess," Sue said, "the corporate ... patron saint of Indiana wants to interview our daughter."

Kristin nodded grimly, besieged by their stares.

Dan smiled at Kristin. "What have you got to lose? I know you're uncertain about what you want to do, but this is a primo-employer."

She waved a dismissive hand in the air. "Hey, you two, everything's under control here. I emailed them a resume before I left Bloomington, figured, 'what could it hurt,' and I completely expect to go for the interview."

There was no point in anyone saying anything more. She was her father's daughter. For several minutes they sat quietly, eating pizza, listening to the wind hiss in the trees overhead.

Sue asked questions about the salvage work and recounted gossip and news about old friends, but Dan had lived with this woman long enough to know she'd come for something beyond sharing lunch. As Sue began talking about the expatriates she'd heard would be back in town for the class reunion, her real purpose was revealed.

"You know Dan, I really don't want to go alone. Won't you please come with me?"

It was the first time she'd suggested they go together.

"Surprised you're not taking Frank Wilson," he said.

"Oh, that would be awkward," Sue said, ignoring his obvious try at making her uncomfortable. "He wouldn't know anybody and I'd end up spending the whole time having to entertain him. These are our friends Dan. Won't you come? We can still have a good time together, there's no reason we can't." The soft, insistent tone of her voice, the most significant voice of his life, was unmistakable. Like any husband of so many years, he knew the cues, the unspoken meaning behind pitch and tone.

As Sue spoke, Kristin knowingly glared at her father, urging him to accept.

Knowing now that Frank Wilson wouldn't be there and that he would be with Sue, a part of Dan really wanted to go, but his pride wouldn't let him appear too eager. He noticed that Kristin's face was now cast down and her eyes closed.

"Kristin, what are you doing?" he asked.

"Praying for divine intervention."

Relenting, Dan smiled at Sue. "Thanks Sue. I'd be glad to go."

They finished their lunch reminiscing about old friends, long since moved away.

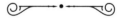

Dan and Kristin pulled the woodwork from around the downstairs windows. Large chunks of plaster came loose and shattered on the floor. The entire outer structure of the house was brick. When the house was built, voids in the mortar joints had been carefully left in areas where nails would hold window trim and baseboard in place. Wood wedges had been whittled, then hammered into the voids, their locations marked with a piece of straw stuck in wet plaster. The trim carpenters then nailed the trim into the wood wedges. The wedges had shrunk over the decades, so as Dan and Kristin pried the trim loose, the nails held fast to the wedges that pulled free of the brick, taking along with it the plaster sandwiched between them. As the dust from the shattering old horsehair plaster got worse, both donned paper dust masks.

From a pair of portable speakers plugged to Dan's phone, a drum crashed and a corkscrew guitar line erupted, followed by the contradictory twang of Lucinda Williams's voice, at once both frail and commanding, echoing through the downstairs rooms.

When they finished pulling loose all the woodwork in the room and the dust had settled, they let their masks fall loose and began prying the nails out of the backside of the wood with nail cutters.

"What do I do if Lilly offers me a job, Daddy?" Kristin asked.

Dan considered the question a moment. "Try to gauge how bad they want you. If they seem eager, act like you're interviewing them to see if they're good enough for you. Ask what kinds of programs they have, you know—maybe they'd pay for you to keep studying at some point. Isn't that what you want? You're afraid to work in some rut, afraid for the learning to end?"

"Yeah. I was thinking that, too. I mean, if they want me to be really good, a bachelor's degree isn't enough."

Dan stopped working and focused on her, raising his eyebrows, he offered in a deep voice, "Paging Dr. Kristin Reynolds?"

She blushed and turned back to her work, "Can you imagine, me with a doctorate?"

"Well, yeah," Dan grinned.

They worked for a half-hour more without talking, but the subject of careers had started Kristin thinking about her father again. She practiced the line several times in her head before trying it for real.

"What really happened when you lost your job?" she asked. "I was off at school and just heard bits and pieces filtered through Mom ... and saw a few newspaper stories about the strike. Why did you lose your job? They hired back nearly everybody else."

They were kneeling on the floor amid a jumbled pile of trim. Dan straddled a long piece of baseboard. Down the hall echoed a guitar and then accordion solo, filling the gap in their conversation. He looked at her for a moment, half considering her question, half straining, pulling back on the shaft of a square nail gripped tightly between the jaws of the nail cutter. The old brittle nail slid halfway out of the splintered hole before snapping in half.

"Ya know, a lot of the stuff you've asked me about ... the marriage ... love ... I'm kinda discovering the meaning, the reasons, the lessons in it all while I explain it to you. But this one, this issue, everything that went wrong—I saw each mistake for exactly what it was as it happened. I'm not saying I could have changed very much of it, but I totally understood the cause, the meaning of all of it."

He slid the walnut trim forward to the next nail and worked at pulling it out through the backside of the board.

His hair was white with plaster dust. His face smudged, too, with the white chalky powder, only a tanned circle where his dust mask had been showed the color of his flesh. This dusting left Kristin thinking he suddenly looked old.

He went on.

"You have to preface this all with the fact that just six months before the trouble at the plant began, your grandfather died. He was the one who drew me into the plant, taught me the ropes, brought me into the skilled trades. I was what I was because of him so his death left a deep hole in me. We had that hundred-year-old house downtown to deal with, the one I grew up in, the one you spent so much time in with them."

"You know," Kristin chimed in, "I never think of them without thinking of that house, that front porch with the gingerbread, those tiny stained glass windows with the flower pattern over the porch and those big, dark, upstairs rooms. I miss that house."

"Well, I tell ya, Sugarcube, after Grandpa died, it was my plan to restore that house, for me and your Mom. She didn't want to, but I think if I'd really pushed her, she'd have gone along with it. But, a couple weeks after the funeral, the city came and made their offer to buy it from me and your aunt and uncle. It was one of those things where they said, 'We'd like to buy it for this price. You don't have to agree to sell, but if you don't, we'll condemn it, and the court will likely set a price lower than this.' In the world of organized crime they call that extortion. At city hall it's called imminent domain.

"Well, you know what happened," he said, shaking his head in dismay, "your aunt and uncle wanted the money, and, what was the point in fighting. And so they tore our home place down to expand city hall so they could service all the new people coming to town, and well, the place where I grew up is where they park city employees now.

"I bring all this up to give you a sense of my state of mind when the trouble started at the factory. I guess you could say the wind had been knocked outta me a little." He slid the baseboard forward again and pried loose a wood wedge and then began on the nail. Dan went on, talking down to the ancient board, only occasionally looking over at Kristin.

"So, it was time to renegotiate our contract and the company had just been bought by the Japanese a year or so earlier. Well, they submit a contract that no fool would sign." He stopped working and began counting off the issues starting with his thumb raised in the air. "It included a reduction in vacation time *and* a reduction in wages." He peeled back a finger for each issue. "On top of that, new workers would not be union workers—so our negotiating numbers would dwindle over time, and their wages would be lower still. Lastly, we'd lose the right to say no to overtime.

"There's no way!" he shrugged, incredulous, "there's absolutely no fuckin' way in hell. Now you expect some of that at the start of negotiations. Not *that* much, but you expect it. Both sides ask for the moon and then over time they both come back down to earth. Hopefully the earth moves and you settle for what's reasonable. But it didn't work out that way this time. We gave in a little and they held firm. We gave a little more, but they held firm. Weeks and months went by and they never budged. That could only mean one thing, especially in the post-Reagan era; they meant to break the union."

"And this is a conservative town, Daddy," Kristin broke in. "'Union' is a dirty word."

"You don't have to tell me that. But people here have never been nasty about it, maybe just a little less supportive than they might be in a real union town. I think most people sympathized with what we were going through."

Dan broke off the next nail and stood to stack the board on the pile in the kitchen, careful to keep the back-to-back, face-to-face arrangement that protected it from scarring the finished side of the wood. He came back and paced the floor, alternately rubbing the back of his neck and gesturing in the air.

"Well, it came to that point where we were going to have to show we were as serious about our side as they were. So it's onto the picket lines and lots of big talk about showing them who really creates the wealth in a company.

"Well, you know how long it went on. And even though the union leaders gave their pep talks about how we were going to prevail, I saw pretty quick what was really happening. You've studied this global economy in college, I'm sure. I accepted it long before everybody else on the picket line did. The truth is I don't think the company could afford to pay us what we'd been getting paid anymore. There was somebody in Mexico willing to work for a fraction of what your grandpa or I got paid. That company was in exactly the position they said they were in. They were either going to get those concessions from us or they were going to close that plant down. Those were the only two options they had ... or go bankrupt.

"But we were union," he shrugged sheepishly, "we were used to being lied to by people wearing suits who were making four times what we made. So this time they were telling the truth, but we'd been lied to so many times over so many years, most still believed it was all a game of who was going to get the dollars. But it wasn't a game; it was a total transformation in what was possible. Thanks to China, and India, and Mexico, the earth had shifted under our feet."

Kristin laid down her hammer and nail cutter, slid back to sit, leaning against the wall. "Well, if you were seeing things so clearly, how is it you were the one left out in the cold."

Dan smiled awkwardly and knelt down over another piece of baseboard. He shrugged his shoulders again. "You'd think that understanding what was happening would have given me some perspective, some motivation to find some other way out for myself, but I couldn't seem to get over the rage. I kept thinking, how could it be that the way of life my father had, and I had, wasn't possible in this place anymore? It had raised two generations in my family—yours and mine. And it was like I wanted somebody to tell me it wasn't true. But it just got more obvious over time. And we'd be out there on the picket line while the scabs and the management guys went in and other fellas are saying things like, 'They'll be sorry,' and, 'We'll turn this thing around,' but I knew in my heart that they wouldn't be sorry and we wouldn't turn things around, and it just stoked my rage."

Dan pulled at another square nail until it broke.

"Well, there was a fella in management, Wayne Dullus, you knew his kids didn't ya? Went to school with 'em? Anyway, Wayne and I had always gotten along. He was one of the management guys who wouldn't hurry past the lines in his big car, pretending not to see us. He'd stop and ask how we all were doing. You know what they always say, 'there're only two bridges across the river in this town. Don't burn either of 'em.' He knew that we all just might end up back in the factory together someday, under some circumstances, and he was keeping the lines of communication open. But after a while his kindness started to grate on me. He'd stop and roll down his window and ask how we were doing and I began coming right up to the window and telling him exactly how we were doing. 'We haven't gotten a paycheck in three months, that's how we're doin'. Did you cash your paycheck this week?'

"Well, that unnerved him, as you'd expect, but he kept stopping, trying to keep things civil, and I kept getting more and more pissed, thinking how things would probably work out fine for him.

"Anyway, one day he stops by the picket lines, bright and early in the morning. The other guys are yelling at the scabs. One of our own drives in, an older fella who needed the money so bad he'd turned his back on his friends and crossed the picket lines, which of course just burned me like nothing else could. Well, Wayne stops his car and rolls down the window and says, 'How you boys getting along?' and I says, 'Sub pay ran out two weeks ago and we ain't been paid regular wages now in six months.' He says, 'I know it's gotta be hard on your families. I hope we get this settled soon so we all can get back to work the way it was before.' And I says, 'I'm sure you got your regular pay last week. It's nice you can keep making payments on your Cadillac. Some of these folks are eatin' out of the Red Cross pantry.' And he comes back with, 'Now Dan, we've always gotten along. There's no reason to be mean. You know I worry 'bout you fellas and want to get past this as much as you do.' And I say back, 'You're driving in there to work while we stand out here. That tells me all I need to know about you.'

"And this was a bad moment for me like you wouldn't believe. That very day he stopped I'd been walking up and down the line stewing over it all, feeling sorry for myself. I was a father, but my kids were gone," he gestured to her. "I was a son, but my folks were dead. I grew up in that house, but the place was torn down. On top of it all I'm walking the street protesting outside the place that had defined who I was as a man. I was outside 'cause they didn't want me inside. I was thinking that things would never be like they once were. Then Wayne Dullus drives up.

"Now, I know he didn't mean any harm by the things he said, and I would like to think that I would be as calm and kind about it if I'd been in his place."

Dan paused and rubbed his chin, "But I wasn't in his place. I was so angry and demoralized. And then he says, 'Dan, I'm not union. If I parked the car and got in the picket line with you boys, I'd never get my job back. *You might*, but I never would. They wouldn't even negotiate with me. I'm doing what I have to do.'"

"And you know, that just pissed me the fuck off! 'Cause, this whole town has lost its soul because of people just 'doin' their jobs,'" he jabbed quotation marks in the air, "and never questioning the way things are done. And I thought of that John Mellancamp song where he sings, 'Callin' it your job, sure don't make it right, if you want me to I'll say a prayer for your soul tonight.'"

Dan pointedly fell silent. He gathered up a piece of baseboard and began working at another nail. "Well," Kristin urged, "what happened?"

Apologetically, Dan said simply, "I hit him."

"You what?" Kristin gushed, incredulous.

"I punched him," Dan said with purposeful nonchalance, "Right through the window of his car. I just punched him."

Kristin stared wide-eyed at him. "I can't believe ... you hit the man? What did he do?"

"Well, we were both a bit stunned. I was lookin' at my fist like, 'How'd that happen?' and all the boys on the line were in shock. Wayne rubbed his chin, raised up his window, and drove away. He never stopped by to talk to us again. He never pressed any charges. Plant security, which had been watching us pretty close, never came out to talk to me."

"Aw Daddy, why did you hit him?" she grimaced, shaking her head.

Dan stared into the floor, shaking his head too, as if to say he didn't know. "I hit him, not because he did anything wrong, I guess ... but I hit him for all these circumstances strung out of control, I was like swingin' at the planets, things far away and outta touch that I'd never be able to change."

Kristin was dumbfounded. "So when the strike ended, Wayne Dullus made sure you didn't get hired back?"

"I guess so. You see, eventually things got so bad, I mean, they hired replacement workers and the more desperate people, those men who were sole breadwinners in their families, they started crossing the picket lines. And well, then, that was all she wrote. It all fell apart—union in disarray. The company offered jobs back to everybody at the new contract *they* mandated—everybody except two guys who were caught dumping nails in the street outside the factory during the strike and ... me."

They were silent a few moments. Dan went on working at pulling nails, but Kristin sat silent, watching him. "I'm sorry, Daddy, that all this happened to you."

"You know, maybe it was best I didn't get hired back. That would have been a tough move to make, to walk back in that factory being totally stripped of dignity and power ... to be beat like that. So maybe it was better this way. I just wish I'd taken the bull by the horns and shifted gears on my own instead of being drawn along by things until I was left out in the cold.

"There are times when the inevitable is so big and obvious, you've got to accept it to really survive. But I didn't. After things got desperate and people started crossing the picket lines, it was so hard to take, like nothing you could ever imagine. For a while there I was above the fray, out of turmoil, looking down on the situation and seeing it for what it was. But I held on to the hope of that job returning and fought against the company and the faithless, too, clinging to the factory and the union and my place in it. And that's what's trapped me.

"It's that way of holding on in desperation that keeps me here I guess. I suppose I could leave town, just drive on beyond the edge of the city limits and make a new life for myself, but I haven't been able to bring myself to do it, even though there's nothing holding me back."

Kristin wasn't really sad. A part of her felt she should be sad to know now how demoralized her father was, but still, she couldn't help feeling her chest expand a little at the recognition that her father was talking to her like an adult, like an intimate equal, worthy of opening up his soul to. She was turning it all over in her head, analyzing the details of her father's troubled life.

"Daddy, I don't understand," Kristin finally said, "with everything falling apart, how could you let Mom slip away? She was the only sure thing left in your life."

Dan laid down his hammer and nail pullers and rubbed the back of his neck with the palm of his hand. He shook his head. "It's ..." He fell silent, searching his mind.

"You know," he went on, shifting gears, "I remember something my father did when I was a kid. I was in the backyard of your grandparents' house. I was maybe ... nine years old, and he was just home from work, watering grass in the backyard. I was playing in the sandbox with little green army men. The sandbox was just a big tractor tire he'd filled with sand. I can remember looking up at him. He was holding the hose in one hand and a bottle of beer in the other, and you know, just winding down from the day.

"Well, a guy drives by in a brand new Corvette. The guy sorta got on the gas as he went by and there was that split second squeal of tires and then it shot off in a flash, my old man and me watching it with absolute lust in our hearts for that machine. Well when I looked over at the driveway and our white Chrysler station wagon sitting there, I knew which one I'd rather have.

"So I'm kinda sulking 'cause we got such a crummy car and I say to my dad, 'I wish I was a grown up. I'd have a neat car to drive like that guy.'

"'It ain't so easy,' he say's back to me.

"'What's so hard 'bout it?' I say back.

"He says to me, 'It's not that easy being a grown up. You think you'll have things a certain way, but it don't work out like that.'   .

"I must have shrugged my shoulders or something, so he tells me to grab a handful of sand and he's going to show me what it means to be an adult. 'Now grab a big handful,' he says, 'because that handful of sand is gonna represent everything you want in life.'

"I grabbed a big fist full.

"'Now that handful of sand represents everything you love,' he says, 'every grain is something you want for yourself.' So then he asks me, 'Who do you love, Danny?' And I thought for a minute and said, 'you and Mom, Grandma and Grandpa.' I named my dog and a couple friends.

"'We're all there in your hand right now. Okay?' he said. Then he asks, 'What do you want to be when you grow up?' And I say I want to be a short stop for the Reds. 'What if that don't work out?' he asks. I said I'd work in the factory with him if I couldn't play for the Reds—I'd be just like him. He asks me where I want to live and what kind of car I want. I tell him I want to live in that house right there with them and that I'd drive a Corvette just like the one that just went by.'

"'It's all there in your hand, Danny,' he says to me. 'Everything you want and things you ain't even grown up enough to know to want yet.'

"Then he grabs my wrist. He says, 'Now everything you want is in your hand, and this water coming out of the hose here represents life comin' at ya, and the passage of time, the forces of the community, the actions of other people in your life, and all your own weaknesses. They're all here in this spray of water.' And he turned that spray of water on my fist.

"At first it wasn't threatening or anything. And it was funny 'cause I was getting all wet and it was a hot day, but pretty soon I could feel water creeping in and getting the sand wet. He let go of my wrist for a moment and twisted the nozzle to narrow the spray of water, then gripped my wrist again and pointed the spray back at my hand. Sand started to ooze out of either end of my fist and he says, 'Better grip it tighter Danny, you're losing some of those things you want so bad.' So I strained my hand to tighten my grip, but that just forced more sand out. I started to get upset, feeling he was making a fool of me. Pretty soon it felt like there was no sand left and I just gave up and opened my palm and the water sprayed the last bits of sand away.

"Then immediately, like I'd broken something precious, my dad twists off the nozzle and drops the hose and grabs my fingers with his hand and quickly curls my fingers back into a fist and says, with a heartfelt passion I almost never heard from him, he says, 'Never let go, Danny. Don't ever let go. You might think there's nothin' left, but there always is. There's always a little something left, even when you think there isn't.'"

Dan fell silent and stared at the wall, a hint of tears just beginning to well up in his eyes.

"So that's what you did with Mom," Kristin put in, "you felt it all slipping away, everything you wanted, everything that told you who you were." She cocked her head to one side, listening within herself for a deeper application of the metaphor. "You lost your faith. It's about faith ... and hope, isn't it ... the lesson he was trying to teach you? It started out as a lesson about being an adult and accepting the limitations of life, but accidentally, when you opened your hand, it became a lesson about hope. He wanted you to have faith that even when things seem empty, there's always something left."

"Yep," Dan nodded. "I guess I lost my faith in this place, and this life."

"And in the value of fixing things with Mom?"

"I guess so."

"But Grandpa was right, there always is something left," she insisted. "Isn't salvage all about hope ... and redemption, the belief that even though things are being torn apart, there are pieces left worth keeping."

He didn't respond, but watched her face, watched the wheels turning behind her eyes, and the words leaping out of her mouth.

"Even though you let go, it's possible to wrap your fingers around something again. Isn't that what you're doing with these houses? Finding your faith and hope again?"

Dan looked down at a scattered pile of broken square nails on the floor, shaking his head and smiling nervously. "I don't know, Sugarcube. Maybe you're confusing hope with desperation?"

"No, Daddy." She gave him a warm smile of encouragement. "You're the salvage man, and salvage is about hope, and redemption."

CHAPTER 11

In the darkness of the surrounding farm buildings, Dan turned off the truck and climbed out. He gazed up at a black sky scattered with stars. Quickly the silence was shattered. Like the thump of a distant earthquake approaching from deep underground, a car passed along the road sending thunderous hip-hop base reverberating through the trees. He shook his head in dismay at the fractured tranquility and moved on past the carriage shed among a chorus of crickets. As he stepped from the dry grass to the fresh black strip of asphalt, Ellen's eyes took him in with deeper examination than on previous nights, as if seeing him anew.

"Hope and redemption," she said flatly.

Dan made no response.

"That wasn't a Sugarcube talkin'," Ellen said, "that was a grown woman."

"Yeah, hard for me to get used to sometimes."

"The tit-for-tat, it's gone in unexpected directions, hasn't it? You tell yer stories to yer daughter for me during the day, and I show you mine at night. She is really more marvelous than I could have ever guessed. She knows what questions to ask—what ones need to be asked to get at somethin'. If it were just me, not knowin' you like she does, I'd just be shootin' blind."

Dan walked on and Ellen followed, along the new black road tattooed with clay-colored muddy tire tracks, into the mostly barren landscape of the new subdivision. Ahead, in the distance, the silhouettes of a handful of model homes defined the far road. Around them, sloping concrete curbs lined dirt lots. Here and there, electric cables jutted out of the ground, bundled together with black tape. They hadn't gotten far when Ellen stopped and eased cautiously backward. Dan, hands in pockets, turned to her. Their eyes met and she shook her head side to side. "I can't go no farther," she said, her hands crossed on her chest.

"But we've walked this way before."

"I, I know," she sputtered. "It's been feelin' a little different lately and it feels quite different now. I can't go no farther in this direction."

Dan raised no complaint or question. They turned back toward the house, through the thick line of trees and shrubbery that temporarily sheltered the farm buildings from the transformation of land to the south. As they reached the edge of the little brick milk house, Ellen offered an explanation.

"I think the activity of people, or the absence of it, gives a place a spirit, a feeling. I caught ya thinkin' 'bout it the day I first revealed myself to you. You felt my presence and remembered other houses that made ya feel invited or unwelcome.

You were feelin' that spirit of place. There's a place where I belong. It has that spirit, that feelin'. It's here," she gestured wide with her arm toward the grouping of buildings, "and it used to be back there, too, in them fields where me and my husband and children and grandchildren worked, where the horses and oxen we fed and loved and tended stomped the ground for years. But I guess that spirit's dyin' out there now. It's been dug up and smoothed 'round, tunneled under and covered over. I don't belong there no more."

Dan started to speak, but she drove on past him.

"And yes, I know, just as you said the other night, that same thing will happen to this stronghold as well." They stopped at the back porch and sat along the edge.

"We're nearly done with the house," Dan said. "We'll start on the barn in a couple days."

She seemed not to be listening. "I had the strangest experience today after ya left. That friend of yers, Tom? He came here 'round the supper hour and waited a while, then a young woman came in another vehicle and he let her into the house. They seemed to be meetin' for the first time. She walked the rooms—seemed to be examining the place, and the whole time I was gettin' this incredible feelin' from her—some connection. It was just so unbelievable. She was completely unaware of the connection, or my presence, but I could feel it so strong.

"You wouldn't believe it Dan, the things yer mind, yer spirit is capable of seein' and knowin', but yer body gets in the way. The friction of blood, the impulses that move muscles, they distract you, impede yer senses. In my state I can see so much, feel information given off by a person, their voice, their features. Anyhow, I figured it out, who this young woman was. She was my great, great, great granddaughter—my Jack's great, great granddaughter."

Dan was caught up in the mystery of her story and the obvious, rare joy it gave Ellen. "But how could you know that?"

"How do ya know when yer happy?" she smiled and shook her head dismissively, "You feel it and ya know it's there.

"Tom followed her while she walked through the house, lookin' in each building, the barn, the carriage shed, the milk house. Then they walked back over there to the family plot," she gestured beyond the trees, "and she examined each stone. On the face of a couple stones, Jack's and my husband's in particular, she laid a piece of paper and rubbed it with a ... I don't know, a piece of charcoal maybe, leaving an image of the stone on the paper."

"Did they talk?" Dan asked.

Ellen nodded, "Yes, but it didn't really mean much to me. Neither was in a high emotional state, so I read little of what they were thinkin'. Tom spread some papers on the front of his vehicle and she said, 'Well, I guess nothing lasts forever.' Then she signed the papers—and here's the odd part; he paid her some money. And that was that. They shook hands, got in their vehicles, and drove away."

"Odd," Dan scowled. "Do you think she's planning to do something with the buildings or maybe she's just doing some research for Tom, considering they named the subdivision after your family?"

Ellen shrugged.

"Could one of your ancestors still have owned the property? Was she signing over ownership?"

"I don't think so. It's been over seventy-five years since I got that connected feeling from anyone who lived or worked or visited here."

Dan stared out at the barn, puzzling over it all.

They were silent a long while. The only sound being the chirping of crickets and the gentle hissing of car tires passing on the road beyond the trees. Dan waited for the feeling to overtake him, for the momentary possession, but instead, she spoke.

"Even after I died, I was a part of Jack's life, for his whole life, until he fell ill as an old man and they took him to town to be cared for. Right after I died, and resisted the crossing over, my soul was in chaos. I could see what was goin' on around me, and move at will, but I didn't know how to communicate with others. It was like learnin' to talk again, to pull together all the spiritual things I was and refocus them into human forms of communication and shapes of bein'."

Then it came to Dan, his own crossing over into her vision, her secondhand memory. He was against the ground, in near pitch-blackness, but slowly, the form of the small boy came into view. It was Jack, the boy he'd walked with to the river and watched sob at his mother's deathbed. He lay in the grass beside a dirt patch, wearing a long white night shirt. It was the middle of the night. The ground was damp with dew. The boy was crying softly. He was lying beside Ellen's grave in the family plot beyond the trees behind the milk house.

Like one's eyes adjusting to darkness, Dan's own mind's eye adjusted as well and Jack's features became more and more clear. But this vision was an otherworldly step beyond normal human perception. This moment came after Ellen's death, after her perspective changed. Though he was look-ing into Jack's face, he had a sense of the view from every angle. The total of the surrounding space had dimension and perspective. He imagined the scene from above the treetops, and then saw it—imagined the scene, standing, behind the child, and was there. These views and perceptions were layered seamlessly over one another like three-dimensional files of effortless memories. He did not feel the damp ground in a temporal way, but somehow knew it was damp, did not feel the cool night air, yet knew it was cool. Information came from outside the normal sensation.

Some direction from Ellen forced his attention squarely on the child. Tears trickled down Jack's cheeks. He sat up, cross-legged and hopelessly, randomly, picked at blades of grass on the ground. In a quick, convulsive burst, he sobbed again, loudly, then beat frantically at his own face with the palms of his hands. He finally dropped his hands to his knees, his chin to his chest, and wept softly.

In the same way that some spiritual barometer informed the dimensions of this scene, there was an otherwise impossible understanding of the child's state of mind, thanks to this view beyond death, through the eyes of a spirit. Loneliness, misery, and rage radiated off the child like heat waves off a sunny summer highway. But in an even further layer of understanding from outside the moment, Dan knew that this was not the point. This moment of hopeless sadness was about something else.

And then something inexplicable happened. The boy fell silent and suddenly alert, as if hearing a distant voice. He turned his head to one side, listening. He stood quickly, looking up at the sky, confused. A hopeful smile crossed his lips and he called out hoarsely, "Mama?" At that moment Dan lost Ellen's vision and was isolated into a more human observance at the edge of the family plot. In a convulsion that jerked his shoulders back, Jack fell to the ground and lay spread eagle on his back. He broke into tears again, but not tears of sadness, tears of long-awaited joy.

The vision faded and Dan was again in the darkness of the back porch beside Ellen.

He turned a disbelieving eye toward her. "You went inside him, didn't you ... inside his body?"

She nodded. "It wasn't my intention, I didn't even know it was possible. But I was a clumsy spirit in those days. It took learnin' to form words in ways that the livin' would understand, to reform myself as I had known myself best, learn to use the spiritual freedom. At that moment you just saw I was tryin' to get close to him, to hold him, to speak to him, to soothe his sadness and tell him that I would never leave his side, and before I knew it, like tripping at the edge of a pond and falling into the water, I was inside of him. There was an exhilaration of comfort and spiritual release that cannot be compared to any earthly experience. But then again, for me it was a welcome earthly experience. I can re-create the experience of the senses, but it's not the same. So, to see and feel the world through him and to be so connected to another human being through the sheer purity of your soul is somethin' that cannot be described and I wouldn't even dare try to take you to the experience. I couldn't re-create it with all its meanings in a vision for you if I tried."

As soon as she said it, Dan thought of the alternative. *Just because she can't show it to me in a vision, doesn't mean she can't do it to me in reality and I perhaps could do nothing to stop her. She could probably just move inside of me at any moment.* The prospect terrified him and she quickly read it.

"Oh no, Dan," she said. "Just 'cause we share these private stories about ourselves, please don't ever think that I'd ever do such a thing to you. That would be an invasion of privacy so complete. You have my word."

"I trust you," Dan said.

"Thank you."

They passed an awkward silence. At some point Dan noticed that Ellen's bundle had appeared again. It always came this way, without warning, and it unnerved him every time. One moment she was there, a single form, sharing her thoughts with him, so normal that she almost seemed a live person, and the next she was silently cradling a baby that never cried and never needed to be fed, reminding him that she was anything but normal.

Dan tried to drive his own focus away from such thoughts. "What would I see?" he blurted, "if I was in the same situation as Jack was then. What would it do to me?"

Ellen smiled at him. "All I know is what I experienced with my boy. All my memories would be available to you at will and all of yours available to me. Our emotions, intentions, sundry thoughts—all laid bare. I would feel your senses— sight, sound, touch, taste—as you do. And you would get a view of my senses as well. You could see the wind blow, recognize the definition of surrounding objects in complete darkness, read the strong radiated emotions of others, feel changes in the weather comin', sense gravity and the hidden shapes within objects. It's so much more than that vision I just showed you."

"That would be miraculous." Dan shook his head in amazement. "It's funny, everybody knows that things have an unseen structure, that gravity holds us to the earth, that the wind blows, that the things that were there in the light are still there in the darkness, but we take the existence of them all on faith, trusting. But to see them or sense them, as you said, that is simply beyond imagination."

Ellen rolled her tongue in her mouth, smirking. "There's a rock on the ground, just in front of your right boot."

Dan looked down at it.

"Pick it up," she said.

Dan did as he was told.

"Throw it at your vehicle," she said.

Dan threw the stone. It hit the tailgate with a metallic clank.

"I can see all those hidden things, those things that have mystified or terrified people for eons, but I can't even pick up a rock and throw it. I can see all the things that make this world work, but I can't do anything with 'em. Helpin' Jack by movin' through him, those were the last times I made any difference in this world. I would gladly give away all these qualities that death makes possible, just to have some meaningful effect on this world again. There is no greater curse, no greater insult to a soul, than bein' invisible and useless."

With the occasional help of the backhoe operator who was digging foundations for Ballard Woods, Dan believed he could take the barn apart piece by piece, leaving the roofing in a pile for Tom's demolition crew and taking the siding and barn timbers for the restaurant.

The skeleton structure of the barn was made of four identical framework sections that each stood two-and-a-half-stories tall. Two supported either end of the barn and the other two lined the central, drive-through bay. The sections were made of eight-inch-square beams cut from hardwoods felled on the farm. They had been hand-hewn with an ax and an adz; their strike marks still visible along the length of each beam. Each section was originally assembled one at a time, raised into place, and then tied together into one structure by long horizontal beams. All the beams were held tightly together by deep mortise and tenon joints, locked together by wooden pegs driven through the joint. This made for a remarkably sturdy structure, three bays wide. The central, drive-through bay opened up completely with sliding doors on either side. The lower east and west bays were fashioned with pens and stalls to house and feed livestock. Above, the hayloft was one large space.

Dan planned to start at the west end. They would remove the siding from the west bay. Then, with the help of an extension ladder and a chain saw, he would sever the joints of the roof supporting and second-floor timbers for just that bay down as far as the hayloft floor, cutting it free from the rest of the structure. He figured it would stand, though precariously. The backhoe operator would then come as needed, using the long arm and bucket to pull the roof structure off that section, leaving a single story of timbers to be safely removed by hand. Dan would move on to the next bay and repeat the process all over again, slowly cutting away the second story of the barn one bay at a time. Granted, this second-story layer of timbers would be a potential sacrifice—some would be saved and others might be destroyed as they fell, but their weight would have to be removed to make it safe enough to dismantle the lower layer of timbers. If he ordered in a crane he could save them all, but would be broke in the end from the expense. He'd measured the inside of the proposed restaurant and felt sure he'd have more than enough beams for Mary Beth Ward.

Dan and Kristin spent an entire day of sunlight on extension ladders removing the siding from the westernmost bay. The following day Dan set up the extension ladder at the far western end of the hayloft and raised it to the uppermost timbers. Using a chain saw he started at the roof and began severing joints. He lowered and moved the ladder along a single plane, using the chainsaw to sever the upper-western one-third of the barn from the rest of the structure. The exposed timbers held fast to one another, but they were no longer connected to the rest of the barn. For the moment they were a free-standing structure resting atop the second floor. Only the roof sheathing bound them to the eastern two bays.

He climbed down, took the ladder out, and asked the backhoe operator to drive over. Once there, the long arm of the backhoe ripped across the roof of that end section, sending the timbers tumbling down along with a splintering, clattering cloud of dust and shingles. Dragging the claw of the bucket as gently as possible across the now-exposed section of hayloft floor, most of the roof debris was pulled onto the ground, bringing the gable timbers along with it. Half survived the fall. The weight of one timber had driven it straight down through the loft floor and to the dirt floor below.

Dan and Kristin climbed up onto the loft floor. At floor level, Dan cut nearly all the way through the vertical beams that remained, pushing them over the edge to crash into the yard. It was exhilarating to stand there within the gash they'd cut. Where the roof had capped the dim space—blue sky shone. The exposed skeleton of the remaining two-thirds of the structure rose up on the east side, cut clean as if God himself had come down and sliced it away. The west side was now exposed to the thick canopy of trees. Still, there was an edge of sadness to it all, knowing they were destroying something irreplaceable.

Kristin stood, hands on hips, watching her father examine the space. Her khaki shorts, white Triton Brewery T-shirt, and face were smudged with dirt. Her blonde hair, tied in a careless knot, gleamed in the bright sunlight. She curled her lower lip out and blew a few loose strands of her bangs from her forehead. "We're rapists," she said.

Dan cast a sidelong glance at her. "Yes. Yes we are."

She looked out toward the sprouting houses to the south. "And nobody comes to the rescue. Nobody cares."

"Oh, somebody cares," her father said, concentrating on a beam lying across the loft floor. He bent and gripped the end, motioning with his head for her to grab the other end. "Let's see if we can push this over to the edge."

They managed to wrestle the eight-inch-by-eight-inch by sixteen-foot-long timber to the north side edge of the loft. Sitting on the floor and using their legs, on the count of three they kicked the timber over the edge and into the soft grass below. Using a chain hooked to the trailer hitch on his truck, they dragged it and the other fallen timbers into a pile at the edge of the drive.

They gathered their tools and cleaned their hands with the ice cold water from a thermos. Tom's Hummer came along the new, curving subdivision road, across its rutted dirt end and into the old gravel drive beside Dan's truck. He hopped out quickly, pulled the sunglasses off his face, and smiled at the cut in the barn.

"Man-o-man, you got it figured out, don'tcha?"

"Worked pretty well," Dan agreed, scrubbing his hands together beneath the trickle of ice water.

Kristin sat on the tailgate of the truck and smiled at Tom.

"Your dad's a pretty smart fella, ain't he?"

"He'll do," she smiled back.

"Gonna hafta do!" Dan laughed, happy with their success.

"Well, you're welcome to the backhoe as long as I can spare it. But next week it's gonna be pretty busy."

"Starting more foundations?" Dan asked.

"A couple, but we've also got the Department of Archeology people scheduled to come in and observe the removal of that little cemetery over there,." Tom pointed beyond the milk house. "Law says they have to gather and label the remains. So I suspect it might be a little slow. Now, we don't have to do it like an archeological dig with brushes and tweezers, thank God, we can just dig it up with the backhoe, but we have to let them gather bones and any other artifacts. They tell me the coffins are probably gone—rotted away ..."

"Wait a minute," Dan said. He wrung the water from his hands, approaching Tom slowly, studying his face. "You're going to dig up that old family graveyard?"

Tom turned back toward the barn. "Yeah. What are there? Twenty plots? It's no biggy, really ..."

"No biggy?" Dan demanded, his face twisted in disbelief.

"Naw, they do it all the time. We'll have to remove the stones ... hey, want one of those old stones? A couple of 'em are pretty fancy—kinda eaten away, but still, pretty fancy. Maybe you could sell 'em at one of those salvage yards you deal with."

Tom turned to Dan and saw the look of horror on his face.

"You can't do it. Now come on Tom," Dan said, walking closer, his voice stern, but uncertain, "you're tearing all this down," he motioned wide toward the house, the grain shed, the garage and milk house, "removing everything—isn't that enough?"

"Look Dan, I know it seems wrong at first—when you first hear about it, but truth is, nobody's been buried there in over a hundred years. I checked. There's nobody alive that knew anybody in that old settler-family buried over there."

"Tom, I'm beggin' you," Dan insisted through clenched teeth, "you mustn't do it!"

Kristin slid off the truck and moved toward her father, concerned by the fear and passion in his trembling voice.

Tom stepped back, unnerved. "Dan, you gotta understand, none of the people who'r gonna buy these houses are gonna want to look out their windows at a graveyard. It'll give their kids nightmares."

"I'll stop ya!" Dan shouted. "It's gotta be illegal. I'll find some way to stop ya!"

Tom shook his head, stunned. He spoke gently, trying to calm his old friend. He pressed outward with his palms, as if to soften the air between them, "Now simmer down a minute here. You can't stop me. I've got a permit from the state. I found a great great granddaughter of somebody buried over there and she signed off on it. That's all Indiana law requires."

"So that's it," Dan spat, "the gal who came and did the rubbings on the gravestones the other day—the gal you paid." Dan paced around in a circle in the dusty dirt ruts, nervously running a hand through his hair.

Tom's mouth fell open. "How did you know ...?"

Dan broke in, "You heartless fucker," he shot back. "You heartless motherfucker!" With that Dan turned around and slammed the tailgate on his truck. "Let's go," he barked at Kristin.

Tom pulled off his sunglasses and gestured angrily with them toward Dan, "You need to get a grip ... you need to get a God-damned hold of yourself!"

Dan slammed his door and twisted the key in a single motion, then tromped the accelerator, spitting dust and gravel on Tom and his shiny Hummer while fishtailing down the driveway.

As they rocketed down Main Street toward town, Kristin sat sideways in the seat, her arm across the seat back, studying her father's expression. There were tears running clean lines down his dirty cheeks.

"Daddy," she whispered, searching his face. "I understand that it's wrong to dig up those graves ... but ..."

"You wouldn't understand," he answered hoarsely.

"Try me," she said.

"They're the rapists," Dan said simply, "not us. They are!"

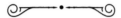

The cut out of the barn cast an ominous silhouette against the gray-black sky. Dan turned off the truck and listened out the window to nothing, listening with his mind, listening for her. His perception of darkness, the one all people come to know in life, had changed. It was no longer a place of hidden dangers, but simply a space of the unknown, not to be feared, but instead filled with knowable contours and locations. Blackness is not simply the absence of light, but a place where a different sort of illumination takes place, thanks to the absence of the distracting nature of light.

And then there it was. Like a light switch casually flipped on he sensed her there in the darkness, there beyond the trees behind the milk house, in a place he had seen from a distance but never explored, where they had never walked—the family plot. Her glowing form came into view in snatches as he moved through the trees. She was there amid the stones, standing bolt upright, her eyes closed, her arms crossed on her chest. A symbolic pose struck once more for him.

Passing into the clearing, he watched her. She dropped her arms and their eyes met. No words were spoken, but the rich, adrenaline rush of understanding passed between them, an understanding of how desperate the situation was.

Soon there would be nothing left of home, no place for her to belong. Not even for a disembodied spirit.

Dotted around them were the stones—some limestone, some sandstone, and one granite—that marked the first and second generations of Ballards on the land. A family forgotten by all in town but a few local historians. Except for the single, tiny granite obelisk, the once smooth surfaces of all the stones had been attacked by over a century of freeze and thaw, sunlight and rain. They were porous slabs, the once sharp edges of words and weeping willows and skyward-pointed hands, now rounded and ill defined, stained calico with green and black patches of lichen and moss.

"The living think of graveyards as the resting place of the dead. It's not really true."

"I've always felt that way, too," Dan replied.

"Graveyards are for the livin', not the dead. What was laid to rest here ain't really me, just my body, which was no longer me before it was laid here. But people want to think their loved ones are there."

"It's how people show respect and remember. It's the only proof you ever lived."

Ellen nodded, "It's the restin' place of *respect* for the dead." She fell silent, gathering new thoughts.

"My gift from God, Jack, never really accepted my death. He would come here and sit in the grass and weep for me. At first he didn't come—wouldn't come—while the dirt was fresh. But the next spring, like the night I showed you, he began bringing crocus, jack-in-the-pulpits, and sweet peas he found in the woods and left them here. He was the only one I spoke to as much as I've spoken to you. I wasn't as adept at it then as I am now, but he knew I was here and I would soothe him with loving thoughts. When he grew to a man he took over the farm. He would bring his children here and came here until he was an old man."

"You never spoke to your husband?" Dan asked gently.

"I did, once. It terrified him. He shrieked and cried and pulled his hair—thought I meant to haunt him instead of comfort him. I wanted to comfort him, but if it was horrifyin', there was no point. So I came to him in the night, in his sleep, and lay beside him in our bed. But then he remarried and he was no longer mine. That bedroom was no longer my place—until *she* died."

"Did you speak with any of them when they passed on? They must have been about, for a moment anyway."

"I came to understand that by resisting the crossing over, at my own death, that I lost a chance of sorts—lost the moment. When my Jack was an old man, I resigned myself to watch for signs of his impending death. As he died, I would come to him completely, in spirit, and cross over with him. But it never happened. I think he died in town. I didn't know he was dead until his body was brought back here."

"Is there no way for you to cross over?" Dan asked.

Ellen was silent for a moment. She finally spoke, "Something about this place grounds my soul—the ancient trees my children climbed, the hand formed brick, this stone bearing my name, the earth my husband and sons tilled. I fit somehow. I told you once that when I move far from the house to the edges of the property I can feel myself comin' apart, scattering. It's the pull ... the pull to the other side."

CHAPTER 12

Dan stayed home later than usual, waiting to see Kristin off. She tried on three different outfits, trying to strike a balance between fashion and conservative business wear. She sat in the car at the curb with the window down, staring at the steering wheel. "Am I doing the right thing?" she asked.

"Sure you are," Dan said. "There's nothing wrong with seeing what they have to offer. You have absolutely nothing to lose."

"What if they offer me a job that's not really what I want? I'll feel obligated to take it." She rested her arm on the door and put her head in her palm. "I'm just so terrified of waking up—thirty-five years old, trapped in a dead-end job."

"You're young. You have the freedom to choose. What bills do you have to pay? There's no gun at your head."

"I know, you're right. But it just feels like it's time for me to move on in life, but I'm afraid of making the wrong choice."

Dan knelt alongside the car. He patted her arm. "Everything's going to be okay. Don't let yourself get railroaded into anything today, leave things open, and we'll talk about it."

She pulled away from the curb half-heartedly. Dan stood and watched her disappear down the street, then gathered his things and went out to the farm, spending the morning securing the structure.

He worried about the remaining portions of the barn. How would severing and removing part of it effect the structural integrity of what remained? He borrowed several come-alongs and bound their cables to vertical timbers crucial to holding the bays together. He pulled the ratchet handles until the cables were taut, holding the ancient wooden joints in place regardless of what contradictory forces his deconstruction might trigger.

While Dan sat on the tailgate of the truck eating his lunch, Kristin's car bounded into the driveway. Swinging around to park, she gave her father a wide, giddy smile.

"They want me to do research," she called through the open window. She switched off the car and got out. "I'd work on a research team. And they'll pay for me to finish my master's and maybe more."

Dan stood up with a smile and reached up with both hands, offering her the same high fives he'd started her on after soccer games at age seven. She slapped his hands and hugged him, laughing at the silliness of it.

"How's the money?" he whispered in her ear.

"Excellent."

He pulled back and looked her in the face, "See? Everything worked out fine." They both sat on the tailgate. "Did you accept?"

"Told 'em I wanted to think about it a couple days—talk it over with my dad."

Dan nodded his head and smiled wide. "I'd call that a slam dunk."

They spent the afternoon stacking the barn siding alongside the saved beams and cleared the site for removal of the next section. In a couple days the whole barn would be just one story tall. At 3 o'clock Dan went home to shower for the reunion. "Careful now, Sugarcube," he waved, pulling out of the driveway. "Don't work too late."

The sun was lower in the late afternoon sky now, below the waving tips of the trees that lined the west side of the barn. With that whole wall blown out, the interior west side and central bay of the barn had been brightly illuminated in a moving stripe of light that began just after noon and for a few hours moved across the dirt floor toward the center of the cavernous shell. But now it was a shadowed place again. The thick line of trees kept the fractured space feeling private.

Working alone now, Kristin dragged old boards, cinder blocks, oil cans, and other trash from the barn floor.

Without the backlit glare of sunlight she now noticed the lines of a loose timber joint she hadn't seen earlier. Where two massive beams met overhead, fastened tight for well over a century by a pegged mortise and tenon joint, the tenon was slipping out of the mortise. The weight or outward pressure pulling it apart must have been great, for it had apparently sheared the wooden pegs meant to lock the joint in place.

At a moment like this her father likely would have urged her out while he secured things, but without him here it was her turn to play hero. She hurried to the come-along that held that two-legged section of timber frame together, spanned some sixteen feet by an overhead horizontal beam. She struggled to pull back on the handle. The ratchet clicked loudly within the metal casing. It took all her strength to pull the handle back a second time. She plucked one of the cables with her thumb and it let out a deep "twong." It was taut, strung between the two upright timbers like a giant guitar string.

Returning to the joint, Kristin recognized progress, but it wasn't tightly back together yet. It needed one more pull on the come-along, but she lacked the muscle.

Looking about the scattered debris on the floor, she mumbled, "I think Archimedes had something to say about this." She quickly found a rusty, three-foot-long pipe. As she slid it over the handle of the come-along the timbers overhead let out a long, threatening groan, like the ghost of some long gone cow baying in its pen.

"Don't worry," she whispered, eyeing the timbers, "we'll put you together just until we need to pull you back apart."

The long pipe combined with the handle to give her leverage, making it easy to twist the cables, turning the ratchet handle from vertical to horizontal while she made another pull.

Kristin pulled on the pipe, doubled over at the waist with arms outstretched, stepping backward. The ratchet clicked like ticks on a clock against the gear. As she strained backward near the end of the arc of the pull, the timbers groaned loudly again.

With a sharp metallic clap and then hiss, the come-along cable snapped. The ratchet housing shot through the air at the end of the unwinding cable and swung in a wide loop about the two timbers. As Kristin fell backward, the metal housing smashed into her lower ribs like the tail of a whip. A frayed end of cable landed with a crack on the side of her head just before she struck the hard ground, the pipe-lever still gripped tightly in her hands.

The timber frame tenon overhead pulled completely out of the mortise while she struggled for consciousness. Her eyes rolled back and she slipped away into blackness as the thunderous sound of wrenching wood and falling timber surrounded her. The floorboards overhead shattered under the weight of the structure as it crumbled in on itself from roof to ground like a hat poked down in the center.

Kristin lay motionless amid a jumble of splintered wood and a century of accumulated dust and decaying hay.

In the distance amid the seedling foundations of the Ballard Woods subdivision model homes, the noise of mortar mixers, air compressors, and radios drowned out the sound of the collapse. The south wall remained intact and only a small tip of the roof betrayed that the north facing wall and roof section had caved in. The line of trees to the north hid even this from all but the most observant of motorist who passed on the road, and even they thought to themselves that the barn was being demolished to make way for the subdivision.

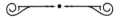

Dan dreaded the reunion. Embarrassed by the place he'd come to in life, he figured everyone else had done better. He was in regular contact with none of them now, none but Tom, and the contempt he felt for Tom was as ripe now as it had been yesterday when he tore out of the farm driveway. And being there with Sue was a mixed bag. On one hand it felt right somehow to be with her while among their old high school friends, yet, she wasn't his wife and the thought of an evening of small talk with her and explaining to those they hadn't seen in years that they were divorced, would be endlessly awkward.

As he and Sue entered the newly built banquet hall in a strip mall on the east side of town, Dan, in the only suit he owned, felt foreign—an imposter. Oldies, '70s-era songs, Motown hits, music he'd grown sick of in the past couple decades, blared from a DJ's sound system. Familiar and half-familiar faces greeted them. But then one face came around a pillar that gave him genuine joy.

It was Gary Burris, who came straight at Dan with a welcome smile and a seeming purpose. "Hopin' I'd run into you," Gary beamed up at Dan. Burris was a portly man with pure white hair, ruddy features, and lively blue eyes, maybe ten years older than Dan and Sue.

"Mr. Burris," Sue smiled, taking his hand.

Gary laughed, "You just had to say the one thing guaranteed to make me feel old."

"It's a nice surprise to see you," Dan added.

"Well, somebody's been kind enough to put me on the list over the years. It's been a long time since I've been down this way, so thought I'd stop in and see people."

Gary had been a young shop teacher during Dan's junior and senior years and they took an immediate liking to each other all those years ago. Gary had hired Dan to help him paint houses over two summers.

"How long's it been since you left here?" Dan asked.

"Well, if it's been thirty years since you graduated, then that makes it about twenty-eight years since we moved up to Warsaw and started the business. Hey, that reminds me, I was hopin' to run into you during the golf outing today."

"I'm not much of a golfer," Dan admitted.

"Well, neither are most of the guys who were out there. When did that ever stop anybody from golfing?"

Sue turned toward another familiar face and Gary nodded toward the bar. "Let me buy you a beer."

Gary and Dan strode to the bar and settled on stools, resting their feet on the long brass rail. "So how's your business?" Dan asked.

"Well, truth is, not so good."

"I'm sorry to hear that."

"Well, as you know, we built a pretty nice little tool and die business up there in Warsaw. Tried to get you to come up and work for us a time or two," he smiled, sliding a beer over to Dan. "At our peak, 'bout two years ago, we had twenty-five employees. We do specialty work—molds, specialty parts, one of a kind pieces, and short run items. We were doin' so well and I was ready to work fewer hours and my oldest son, Ken, had worked side by side with me since gettin' out of college. So I turned the day-to-day operations of the place over to him. Beth and me bought a motor home and we started traveling. Over the last couple years I'd pop in and work a bit, maybe averaged a couple days a week when we were home, but mostly tried to let Ken run the show, make the business his, if you know what I mean, but be there to help out when needed."

"Sounds like a nice situation. What went wrong?"

"Ken never had a knack for the business the way I did. He was good at managing the employees and actually doing the production, but he never liked to work the clientele and didn't have a head for the financial end. But I figured he'd grow into it, ya know, adapt as needed. Maybe I was just kiddin' myself.

"Anyway, couple months ago I got some personal calls at home from long-term clients just pissed-off to beat the band about late orders. I had a long sit down with Ken and then another long sit down with the office manager and between the two of 'em find out that Ken had pretty much run the business into the ground. He was embarrassed to tell me, figured he figure it all out eventually. Office manager didn't want to tell me—divided loyalties and all that.

"So I sit down with my boy and tell him how it's gonna have to be. Well, that hurt his pride, didn't want his old man treatin' him like a little kid, so he walks out." Gary leaned back and shrugged his shoulders, "So here I am, happily semi-retired and I've suddenly got the worst kinda full-time job I ever had, trying to rebuild something I already spent twenty-five years building."

Dan shook his head, "Aw, I'm sure sorry to hear that, Gary."

"Well, good," Gary laughed, staring Dan in the eye, "because I need your help."

"What could I possibly do?"

"Look, at the golf outing somebody told me you were out of work."

"I'm not out of work," Dan shot back, turning to look into his beer bottle. "I do architectural salvage."

Gary shook his head and raised a hand, knowing he'd touched on a delicate nerve. "I'm sorry, I misspoke. You're an independent contractor. But here's my pitch, okay? You're a skilled trades man from way back—the best. I know you know how to weld and run a metal lathe, 'cause I taught you myself. If you want a steady job and a good paycheck and some benefits, I need you Dan. Kenny was my right-hand man for years. He was the one who could walk the floor and know if things were gettin' done right—quality control, you know what I mean?"

Dan nodded.

"But he's done now. Found a job elsewhere, swears he's never coming back to work for the old man, and quite frankly, I don't think his pride would ever let him come back. But a guy like you," Gary pointed at Dan, "could do that job. I can handle the business side," he gestured toward himself, "but I can't run the floor, too. I need somebody like you, somebody who knows how the machines work, knows how to fix 'em if they don't, knows what the final product is supposed to look like and isn't afraid to get his hands dirty in the process."

Dan was dumbfounded. "Jesus-shit, that's quite an offer, Gary."

"Now I don't want to sugarcoat it. We're in a mess. There'll be some long hours. We need to knock some people's socks off by turning a whole bunch of jobs around faster than they've ever been turned around. And I've lost a couple people. They thought the boat was sinkin' and they went and took new jobs."

"Ya know, I've never lived anywhere else," Dan said, staring into his beer. "I've lived my whole life in this town."

"It might be good for ya," Gary said, slapping the bar with the palm of his hand. He took a business card out of his wallet and slid it across the bar to Dan. "I'll make it worth your while. Think about it and give me a call on my mobile, okay."

Dan smiled and nodded.

"Hey, I see somebody over there I wanna to talk to," Gary said, getting up. "Call me, okay?"

The Temptations' "Ain't too Proud to Beg" blared from the DJ's sound system. A few couples had started to dance.

Dan shook his head in exasperation at hearing the song for what seemed like the millionth time. He strode over to the DJ's table.

"Can I play you something in particular?" the DJ shouted over the mixing board.

"Yeah," Dan yelled back, "got any alternative country —Americana?"

"For this crowd?" the DJ shouted, adjusting headphones around his neck. He didn't really want that kind of music at this event, but flipped through his playlists anyway. "Think I've got some Mavericks. Does that count?" Dan leaned over the table and squinted into the computer screen, eventually pointing to "True Love Ways."

The DJ nodded, "The Mavericks doin' an old Buddy Holly song. We're due for a slow dance."

Dan smiled. "Thanks."

He found Sue among a crowd of old friends and took her hand from behind, surprising her. "Dance with me," he whispered into her ear. She was taken off guard and gave him a coy smile.

"Who me?"

Just as the Temptations faded, they reached the dance floor. Raul Malo's achingly smooth tenor filled the room, a cappella, in slow, measured steps.

In the spreading darkness of twilight Kristin woke. Dried blood in one eye matted the lid shut. As she tried to move her arm to wipe it with her hand, excruciating pain shot through her rib cage. She moaned, then lay still a minute, scanning her surroundings with the open eye, trying to gather her wits. Everything that happened was clear in her mind; the cable breaking, the handle and housing of the come-along ratchet striking her chest, the cable across the face and the scream of cracking wood as everything went black. She gingerly tried to lift her head but managed only an inch or two before bumping it against a board.

She was completely covered with lumber and dry-rotted wood and hay. The separating timbers that started the collapse had fallen in an elongated pyramid overhead, protecting her from the heavier debris of other timbers and roofing. One of her arms was pinned underneath her, the other caused blinding pain to move. Kristin was trapped.

She lay motionless trying to think what to do. Beyond her shattered surrounding was only blackness and the sound of crickets. Panic grew at the edges of weariness. She fought against the fear, wanting only to sleep.

She began to drift off again, but was startled awake by a voice that seemed to call, "Are you alright?" She struggled to awareness, uncertain if she had dreamed the voice or heard it for real. She strained her eyes against the darkness.

"Are you alright?" the voice called out again, urgent with concern. It was a woman's voice. Kristin heard it crystal clear, like the ringing of a bell.

"I'm here," Kristin called, lifting her head up against the board. "Help me, please, help me."

Silence.

Did she hear a worried sigh beyond the debris? "Hello?" Kristin called out, confused.

"Yes, I'm still here," the voice said.

"Help me, please," Kristin cried.

"I can't," came the reply, desperate apology in its tone.

"Call for help! Call 911!" Kristin pleaded.

"I can't."

The cell phone on the dash of Kristin's car gave out a delicate, two-note whistle and its screen awoke. Ellen looked over her shoulder at the suddenly illuminated windshield. "There's a cricket in your car," she chirped lightly. She stood and walked to the car, peering through the windshield to examine the device. Seeing words on its screen, she cocked her head to one side to read them just as it went black.

"It reads, 'Where you at, girlfriend?'"

Kristin was confused. Her neck muscles ached from the straining. She laid her head back on the ground and began to cry. "Why won't you help me? Who are you?"

Silence.

"PLEASE DON'T LEAVE ME HERE!" she screamed in desperation.

Silence.

Kristin wept. *What's wrong with this world* she wondered? *How could you not help me?* But then a thought crossed her mind; how could anyone besides her father guess she was there in the darkness and filth and wood scraps? Who was this woman? Something wasn't right.

Her cell phone began ringing. "Pick it up and answer!" she shouted. "Please! Tell whoever it is that I need help!"

There was no answer. The phone continued ringing, then fell silent.

It was too strange, too confusing. She fell into tears again.

Suddenly Kristin felt a cool, soft, yet insistent pressure on her eyelid, a cold thumb gently massaging the tears into the dried blood to free it. She opened both eyes and tried to focus. A shimmering, kind face stared back, just inches from her nose. The woman's body seemed to be woven amid the debris, right up against her own.

Like her father before her, Kristin wondered about her own sanity. The sudden appearance of this kindly, otherworldly face within the seemingly impenetrable piles of wood shook her to her core. Kristin sobbed, "I'm dead, aren't I. I'm dead!" she cried.

"No, no," Ellen cooed as softly as she could, "no, yer alive alright."

"Who are you?"

"A friend of yer father's."

Kristin felt the coolness and pressure move to her shoulder. This apparition was caressing her arm, trying to comfort her, but it didn't feel right, it was too icy and made her arm tingle as if on the edge of falling asleep. This woman did not look right, in fact was *not* right and Kristin knew it. There were layers to her form, like the shape of a real person with an iridescent facade. She wondered if she were dreaming or hallucinating.

The woman raised her hand to Kristin's face and swept the hair back with a finger. The finger slid softly across Kristin's face, cold and tingling like an electrified ice cube. Unnerved, she was seized with fear and began to cry again. She saw the apparition's expression turn from comfort to frustration, then resignation. Suddenly, it disappeared. All was black again.

CHAPTER 13

An hour after dinner, Dan and Sue found themselves sitting on tall stools along a bar that faced two tables crowded with old high school friends and their spouses. They relived old memories and lamented those who were missing. Eventually the conversation turned to the avalanche of growth and change that had come to the once small river town over the past thirty years.

Phil broke in, "I don't know ... I don't mean to trash my own hometown, it's just that it doesn't *seem* like my hometown anymore, it's a different place. Not much is that familiar to me anymore. I know things change, I mean, what place is like it was thirty years ago? But most places haven't changed quite this drastically. Seems whoever's been in charge the past couple decades hasn't planned very well. They let too much growth happen too fast. They had their foot hard on the throttle but couldn't find the brake."

Not everyone recognized that the conversation was an affront to Tom and what he did for a living. As Hoosiers will, those who still knew Tom well enough to know he earned a direct living off that growth said nothing but listened politely, hoping the conversation vandals would quickly come to their senses. Tom, too, was silent, irritated, waiting for the conversation to turn another direction.

"It don't feel like my town anymore either—don't feel like my home," Dan offered softly.

Tom's pride got the best of him. The sting of Dan's attack yesterday at the Ballard farm was still fresh. He shook his head and snorted emphatically, quickly blustering a sentence as if it had been drawn back and flung from a slingshot: "All the growth ever did was make this town rich!"

A hush fell over the group as all now realized, whether they agreed with him or not, that Tom was offended. Dan would have none of it. Even though Sue laid her hand firmly on his wrist as if to say, "Just let it go," Dan stood uneasily.

"Phil," Dan said, "where's that wonderful old brick Victorian elementary school building we both learned our ABCs in?"

Phil pursed his lips, thinking it through. "It was demolished and they built a new one during the first wave of growth ... some thirty years ago."

Dan nodded his head. "Dave," he said, turning to the other side of the crowd and an old friend who was tilted back in a chair and holding a bottle of beer, "where's the roller skating rink we all went to every weekend all the way through high school?"

"Torn down. Replaced by a Hardee's hamburger joint and CVS."

"Sue," Dan went on, "where's the high school we all graduated from?"

"Dan, don't do this," she said gently, pleadingly. But several beers had loosened his tongue and her plea only bolstered his resolve.

"Well, if you're too polite to state the obvious," he said, his voice turning sarcastic, "as unfortunately most of us Hoosiers are, you'd say it was torn down so a bigger one could be built to accommodate more students. And even that has been abandoned and still another one has been built. Hell, the high school we all graduated from is two building generations gone. And I read in the paper recently that now even the newest one will be overflowing in a few years.

"Sue, you'll at least tell 'em what happened to my parents' house, the one I grew up in, won't ya?" Sue didn't respond, but stared back in anguished silence.

"It got torn down," Dan answered for her. "The city took it—imminent domain—and expanded city hall.

"And Brian," Dan turned to a former fellow union member, "What happened to the good union jobs we had."

"The company busted the union," Brian offered easily, agreeing with the point Dan was making.

Dan's tone was rising. He shoved both hands in his pockets, forcing the tails of his sport coat to his sides. He turned and lowered his gaze to Ted. "And where's your family farm, Ted? God, it was such a beautiful place—like a picture postcard."

"We're standing on part of it right now and you know it," Ted barked defensively.

Dan cut in loudly, "Along with a McDonalds and an auto-parts store. Have you been to your old family burial plot lately? It's right behind this building, ain't it? Your ancestors who tilled this land for generations are still there, their gravestones wedged right between the dumpster pick-up side of a strip mall and a football field. But you got your money, didn't you? Moved out west to a place that still had countryside left."

Dan's outburst had taken everyone off guard. He'd insulted his wife and his two best childhood friends. This normally quiet man had lashed out with purpose and painful accuracy.

"And Donna," Dan pulled his hands from his pockets, turning and pointing at a woman who had grown up on the same street as him forty years earlier, "where's the movie theater, the drug stores, the grocery stores ... hell, all the other small businesses owned by people we all knew when we were growing up?"

"They're gone, Dan," she replied quickly. "They're nearly all gone."

"Where's the businesses now and who owns 'em?"

Donna looked uneasily at Tom and then Ted. "They're all out on the highway or in a strip mall ... places like this ... and all owned by out of town or out of state corporations I guess."

Dan looked uneasily at Tom. "Where's that beautiful old church we both prayed in as kids. Remember walking down the aisles with me in those robes accolyting when we were ten? A part of me died when they tore that one down and put a drive-thru bank in its place. That one thing killed that whole neighborhood. It hasn't been the same since. It was the biggest church in town, but too small for a growing congregation. Had to make room for all those new folks you were bringing to town, didn't we Tom?

"And hell, what are the odds that any of us could drive from one end of town to the other and see somebody we know? Not very good."

Dan jabbed his finger in Tom's face. "That's all the growth ever did to our town!" he pointed, "that's all it ever did—destroy everything we grew up with, everything we knew," he jabbed again, "and how we all fit into it. *That's* all it ever did," he jabbed again angrily.

Tom, red faced, stood and forced his chest out, sputtering, "Just ... just 'cause your life sucks, ain't my fault."

"Aw, don't put it back to me, Tom," Dan sneered. "It's people like you who've invited better'n twenty-five thousand people to town since we graduated. That's what's changed everything. But it doesn't matter to you how people feel about where they live. You'll just bulldoze it down and sell the pieces to strangers."

Tom grimaced, his eyes narrowed on Dan, "And I tried to help you. Well ... you're welcome, Dan," he spat sarcastically, pointing back at him. "And ... anyway, I may be changing things for a living, but you're the one who's ripping things up for money, too, and for chump-change at that. Maybe you're just jealous. Don't you see? We're both in the same business, but I'm at the top of the food chain and you're a bottom feeder. And don't forget," Tom moved toward Dan, leading with his shoulder, "you're the one who blew your job. You're the one who blew your marriage."

Tom glared at Dan, breathing heavily like an out of shape prizefighter, ready for a return blow. The group watched Dan's expression, stunned by his outburst, heartsick watching him unravel. Dan looked from the floor to random faces, a mixture of anger and embarrassment.

"You're right," Dan said, shaking his head. "Those two big things, yeah, they're my fault. Yeah, I did some stupid things and painted myself in a corner. But I don't know how to separate what I did wrong from what you do wrong every day. One acts on the other," he pointed from Tom to himself, "one feeds the other. I'm just trying to say I feel lost. I can't find my way."

Dan's voice was on the edge of pleading now, moving from face to face, looking for understanding. "Most of you have all moved on to Chicago, Atlanta, Vegas ... so you guys can call me backwoods or a country bumpkin if you want, but I liked our little town the way it was. I knew who I was back then. And you all knew who I was. People knew each other. When a person screwed up, when a person hit hard times, there was a ..." Dan cupped his hands, molding some unseen force, "there was ... some sorta structure here that gave you a soft landing. You know, if things fell apart for ya, everything else was still in its place ... the school, the church, the stores, the whole town of people. But if something goes wrong now ..." the pitch of his voice rose up nearly to a whine, "you're on your own, buddy.

"I'm not afraid of new people," he lowered his voice, slowing down, looking squarely at Tom. "That's fine to have new people. But not if you got so many that you can't find a familiar face, where all your connections get so watered down that you can't reach out and connect again."

He looked on the edge of tears. "Don't you see Tom," he stepped forward, gesturing toward his old friend, who eased back in defense, "I used to be that guy who grew up in that house, but the house has been torn down. I used to be that guy who went to that school, but it's gone now. I used to be that guy who worshiped in that church, but the church is gone. I used to be the guy who had that good job, but the job's gone. I used to be a father, but my kids have grown. I used to be a husband, but I let my wife slip away. I used to be able to walk down these streets and see an endless stream of familiar faces that helped hold it all together, but now all I see are strangers.

"Who am I?" He shrugged his shoulders and opened his arms wide to the group of old friends. Some shared expressions of sympathy. Others looked away. "Who am I? Are there any clues ... any evidence?" His eyes grew misty as he heard Sue gently crying, sitting on a barstool behind him. "I ... I don't exist," he stammered. "I'm a ghost. I might as well be dead."

Even Tom was moved enough not to attack in response. Softly but emphatically, as gently as his own anger would allow him, he said through clenched teeth, "It's not my fault."

Dan sighed abruptly. "Yeah, but I reach out for evidence to tell me who I am, a clue to tell me where I belong, and you're one of the guys bulldozing all the evidence, hiding all the clues."

Tom shook his head, turned, and walked away.

Dan turned toward Sue, rubbing the back of his neck with the palm of his hand. Tears streamed down her face.

"When did you learn to talk?" she whispered, trying to hold back a sob. Then again, louder, searching and demanding, with an edge of accusation, "When did you finally learn to talk?"

The crowd awkwardly dispersed. Someone tried to pat Dan's back and tell him everything would be okay, but he pulled away and quickly walked out the front door and into the parking lot.

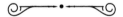

Kristin strained her eyes, searching for some sense of reality. She moved her head about, but could see little more than glimpses of light—a car passing on the road beyond the trees. She was awake and aware and something was out there, she felt it somehow. She tried to compose herself, to force her clouded mind toward reality. The cell phone lying on the dashboard of her car rang in the driveway beyond. She listened to it run through its cycle and then fall silent, then thirty seconds later came the chirp of a voice-mail alert.

"Are you still there?" Kristin called in a hoarse voice.

"Yes," came the simple reply.

"I'm thirsty," Kristin said, not sure what would happen. There was no answer beyond the debris. A few moments later she heard a hollow, plastic echo, what sounded like the cooler tipped over and the lid tumbling off. Then came the sound of a persistent scratching, as if something small was being dragged across the grass. Her eyes were adjusting and beginning to make out the dim outlines of her surroundings. The sliding, scratching sound became a faint clattering of wood scraps, getting closer and closer. She held her breath.

With a start she made out the faint outline of the plastic cap of her half empty water bottle move into place before her. It had been slid along the ground, through the twisted maze of splintered wood, seemingly unaided.

Confusion.

She tried to move her arm to grasp the bottle, but a dagger of pain shot through her chest again. She moaned out loud.

What to do, she wondered, gazing down helplessly at the bottle cap.

"Um," the voice came again from beyond the darkness, "grip it between yer teeth."

Driven by overpowering thirst, Kristin acted on faith, craning her neck far enough to reach the cap of the plastic bottle with her lips. She pulled it into her mouth and gripped it with her front teeth. Soon she felt the bottle beyond the cap twisting, unscrewing itself. The cap came lose in her mouth, the threaded bottleneck resting on her lower teeth. She moved the cap out of the way with her tongue, regripped the mouth of the bottle between her teeth and turned her head back, draining the remainder of the bottle into her mouth.

Kristin spat the empty bottle away and gasped a deep breath. She lay in the darkness, breathing heavily, trying to reason through what had just happened.

"I'm sorry I can't help ya more. You just witnessed the most I'm capable of doing for you."

"Why?"

"I'm just not able."

"They won't find me until morning," Kristin said, straining her eyes beyond the web of splintered wood. In the gaps she could now make out the form of the woman pacing at the edge of the debris pile. Her long dress, her tightly knotted bun, her warm face—all of her shimmering gently. She appeared to be wringing her hands nervously as she spoke.

"No, don't worry, yer father will come soon, he always does, every night."

Kristin didn't answer immediately, but watched the glowing form through the open slits.

Every night? she wondered silently to herself. *So this is where he goes.*

"Yes," the woman answered out loud, turning in Kristin's direction, "we talk each night."

Kristin's eyes met Ellen's through an open gap in the shattered timbers. The figure's intense stare knowingly confirmed what Kristin was trying to understand, that the apparition had responded to a thought, not a spoken question.

Separated by less than twenty feet and a pile of timber, the two women stared at each other.

Adrenaline raced through Kristin's veins. The mist of pain and confusion was suddenly gone. Terrified again, Kristin thought she had never been so acutely aware of a moment before. Only the lonely sound of crickets, only the pungent smell of rotted wood and straw. With her eyes focused squarely on the gently glowing apparition beyond the debris, a pure thought entered Kristin's mind, *"Kristin, my name is Ellen."*

"Oh my God," Kristin cried softly, convulsively, gasping for air.

Once outside the banquet hall Dan cut behind the building and walked the grass path along the drainage ditch between the dumpsters and loading docks of the strip's center to the south and the football field to the north, past Ted's family plot, between the late-1970s school buildings, and finally into the old neighborhoods of town.

He walked, brooding, through the dark streets, beneath the streetlights and the tree-lined sidewalks, his hands in his pockets. What just happened in the banquet hall was painful, but not horrific. He'd been so humiliated over the past several years, spent so much time as the odd man out, that he'd become a little numb to the hurt. In truth, it was an almost cleansing moment of honesty.

He reached 16th Street and was just a couple blocks from Sue's house and his truck parked ahead at the curb when Sue's car idled up behind him. The passenger window down, her makeup run by tears, she blurted out to him, "When did you learn to talk?" He stared back at her. She shouted once more, "When did you learn how to talk?"

He opened the door and sat down. "Sorry I made a scene back there," he mumbled.

She drove on toward the house. "Where was all that when I needed to hear it?" Tears began to flow again. "I tried so hard to get you to open up," she beat the steering wheel with the palm of her hand, "to save our marriage, to get you to tell me what was going on in your head! And now you're blubbering it all to Kristin and then a room full of people ..."

She pulled into the drive, slammed the car into park, and twisted the key off. "Where's mine, Dan?" she cried, jabbing a knotted fist of fingers at her chest. "Now that you've learned how to talk, when are you going to talk to me?"

"I know, I know," he said gently, patting her arm, "you have every right to be angry."

"This is your last chance, Dan," her voice trembled, "your last chance to settle things with me, the last time I'll care to listen. I'm tired of wondering, tired of hurting. I want a life. You obviously can't or won't give that to me. Once I was ... but I'm not waiting anymore."

"I'm so sorry," he said, putting his arms around her.

Sue buried her face in his neck and cried. "I know you said a lot of that back there for me to hear. I understand it and I felt it too, years ago, without really being able to put it into words, but where did *we* fit in to all that? Why couldn't our marriage be the one place where you belonged?"

"Aw, Sue," he sighed, holding her tight, whispering in her ear through clenched teeth, "if I could have admitted it to myself, I would have recognized that I wanted you back, but there were so many things I wanted back that not having the rest of them kinda canceled out the value of having you, made having you a negative thing ... a reminder of all that was lost, everything I wasn't anymore." He took a deep breath, calmed, and continued. "So I let the divorce happen. I wouldn't have taken the initiative on my own, didn't want to. But since you did, I wasn't gonna beg. It was dumb, I know. But it wasn't some macho response to you filing, it was just a sad recognition that I wasn't the man I used to be ... hell, nothing is like it used to be. If anyone had had the guts to ask me why I gave in to the divorce without so much as a complaint, I'd have said, 'Why cry about it? If it's gonna happen, it's gonna happen.' But that wasn't true."

He pulled away and sat upright, looking at her, "By the time I lost my job the kids were off to college, you had a great job, hell, made more money than me. There you were making a good living ... a reminder to me that I wasn't. You adapted to what this town's become and I didn't." He shook his head apologetically, "You were just doin' what you needed to do, I know, but it was just in my face all the time. We'd already lost each other over the years and now there was this financial wedge driven between us that I was too proud to get over. When you add it all up, I lost myself."

"You're such a strong man, Dan, such a good man, how could that happen?"

"I'm not so tough. Delicate things must be carefully kept ... but almost never are."

They sat a few moments in awkward silence.

"I wish there was something more I could say. There ought to be a word bigger than 'sorry,' but I don't know one."

"No," she shushed him, looking away, "there's no point in apologies now."

Sue stared blankly out the open window. "Are you going to take the job Gary Burris offered you?"

"How did you ...?"

"He told me, actually called me yesterday."

"You asked him to come here and offer me that job?"

"He was going to do it regardless. This just gave him an opportunity to track you down. So, are you going to take it?"

"I don't know," he said, shaking his head. "Feel like I should."

"You should," she said quickly. "It would be good for you."

"You said this was my last chance to settle things with you. What does that mean?"

"Frank Wilson asked me to marry him," she offered bluntly.

There was a long silence.

"And?" Dan prodded soberly.

"And I intend to say yes." She turned to him. "I want to have a life and I don't want to do it alone. Maybe this is our chance, Dan, a chance for both of us to move on. We've both been stuck in limbo, trapped by old habits and ... obsolete attachments. Maybe it's time to reinvent ourselves and stop holding onto things that are gone."

Dan was hurt. It stung. But he knew she was right.

"Delicate things must be carefully kept," she repeated his line, "but almost never are. You're right. People are that way. But when they get broken, maybe, sometimes, you have to let go of the idea of putting things back together. Sometimes when things get broken, there's no way to put them back the way they were before, no matter how much we may want it."

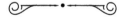

Dan pulled into his driveway, noticing that Kristin's car was not there. Once inside he pulled off his tie and settled down on the couch, thinking he would change before driving out to speak with Ellen. Passing through the bathroom, the laundry room, and the bedroom, he noticed there was no sign Kristin had been there. He lifted the lid on the washing machine. Only his work clothes from earlier that day. This was not their routine. She always started the washer at the end of the day after she put her work clothes in.

He went to the bathroom. The shower was dry. Felt her towel. Dry.

He dialed Kristin's cell phone number. No answer. He dialed Sue's number but got voice mail.

Five minutes later he was pounding on the door of the 16th Street house.

"Is Kristin here?" he asked breathlessly, as Sue opened the door. Her makeup was half off and a hand towel hung over her shoulder.

"No, isn't she out with friends?"

"S'posed to be, but there aren't any of her dirty clothes at my place, no sign she came back. I was hopin' she came here to change instead."

Sue searched his face, taking in the rapid-fire words. "She hasn't been here. The house is just as I left it."

"Maybe it's nothing. But I'm gonna go check the barn out there, just to make sure nothing's happened."

Dan jumped off the front step and ran back toward the truck.

"I'm coming with you," Sue yelled, pushing through the door.

CHAPTER 14

Kristin listened, tormented, as her cell phone rang uselessly once more.

Suddenly Ellen reappeared near Kristin, sitting on her knees within a void in the debris pile. "He's coming," Ellen whispered urgently, nodding her head up and down, pointing with an outstretched arm toward the road. "He's almost here, I can feel him. Don't worry."

"How can you know that?" Kristin demanded. "What are you?"

"It's too much to explain," she sighed, shaking her head, "I just do ... I just am."

In the truck moving north on Main, Dan craned his head to one side as if listening to a distant sound. "No, no, no, no," he began to mumble under his breath, shaking his head.

"What?" Sue asked.

"Something bad happened."

"How do you know?" she asked, shaking her head. "You can't know that. You're jumping to conclusions."

Dan patiently ignored her disbelief, reaching across the seat and squeezing her hand, "She's in danger, but she's alright."

Sue looked back at him as they made the big curve to the east, puzzling at his prophecy. This wasn't like him.

Dan slowed and eased into the drive. As soon as Kristin's car came into view, so did the shattered barn.

As the headlights scattered through the fractured space, Kristin watched Ellen's shape transform in moving shards from gentle glow to transparent glass; its edges barely visible.

She turned to Kristin with intense eyes. "He's not alone," she said quickly as the truck came near. "I'll have to go. But don't worry, I'll be watchin'." She disappeared into the light.

Dan's heart sank as he clicked the brights, illuminating the concave sweep of the crumpled, green roof. The far wall was still standing and the roof held at the wall's top along the eaves, then fell sharply, inverted, to just a few feet off the ground. The near wall was missing, completely buckled under the pile.

Sue screamed out, "No, oh no!"

Jerking to a stop, Dan reached out and gripped Sue's arm. "She's in there, but she's alright."

He pulled a flashlight from under the seat and they both leapt from the truck.

"D-a-d-d-y," Kristin called loud and long.

Sue let out a startled scream. "She's alive. Dan, she's alive, just like you said."

He dropped to his knees under the lip of the collapsed roof and pointed the flashlight within. Some twenty feet ahead between fallen timbers and splintered floorboards he saw her. Kristin, her face dirty and forlorn, squinted back at the beam of light.

"Oh God, Oh God, Oh God," Sue whimpered softly, "baby are you alright?"

"Quiet!" Dan hissed.

He pointed the light beyond Kristin's face, trying to get a glimpse of the rest of her body. "Tell me, Sugarcube, how are you?"

"I'm okay, I think. Is there an opening where you can reach me?"

Dan examined the debris pile, pointing the beam of light about. "Boy I don't see how."

"Well, you've got tools and things here," Sue broke in, frantic, "we'll saw and chop and hammer our way to her."

He held a hand up to quiet her. "Kristin, are you bleeding … or is your circulation cut off anywhere?"

"No, I'm just trapped, things have fallen so close around me I can't move. But Daddy, there's something else."

"What."

"Someone has been here to see me, to talk to me. But she's gone now."

Dan didn't respond, he knew who she meant.

"A woman," Kristin went on. "But she's not normal. She appears and disappears. And she says she knows you."

"Has she tried to comfort you?" he asked, a mist of emotion building in his eyes.

"She's tried, but I'm afraid."

Sue gripped Dan's shirtsleeve tightly, "Don't you see what's happening here?" she whispered urgently, near hysterics. She'd had enough of his calm, measured approach. "She's dying. She's having one of those near-death experiences you hear about. She's not okay! We've got to get her out and to a hospital."

Dan's mind read caution. "No. Let's look this over and figure out the best way to handle it. We need to think this through."

Sue would have none of it. "Dammit Dan," she growled. Sue leaned forward on her knees, tucked her head under the fallen eves and began tearing at the scattered debris on the ground.

In Ellen's world of awareness, where weight emits wave-like dimension and physical pressure bleeds color, the danger Kristin was in was quite clear. Ellen shared this vision with Dan and he understood.

He tugged at Sue's arm. She tore away with a frantic, "No," continuing to yank on boards and shattered siding. From behind, Dan grabbed her around the chest with both arms and pulled her back on top of him. In the glaring light of the truck's headlights he maneuvered himself on top of her, on his knees straddling her, gripping her wrists tightly.

"Stop! Listen to me," he shouted into her face. "It's gonna fall on her if we pull the wrong thing out! There's several tons hanging in the air above her!"

Sue stopped resisting and lay silent, looking up at him. His words rang in the air, only their heavy breath broke the silence.

"We need the police, and the fire department," he said more softly but pointedly.

She nodded in understanding.

"Okay ... okay. You call 911 and I'll start trying to figure this out."

He got up and stepped back. Sue scrambled to her feet. Dan pulled his cell phone from his pocket and handed it to her. Sue dialed desperately while Dan ran to the back of the fallen structure.

Ellen was there, in full form, when he reached the other side. Their eyes met but Dan did not speak or think of anything but Kristin. He peered in through another broken opening. Ellen knelt beside him and they both looked in at Kristin.

Kristin's dirty, forlorn face met theirs. "What's happening, Daddy?" she asked, looking at Ellen, feeling the unrealness of the moment, being trapped, hurt, and in danger, and searching out at the alien beside her father. Perhaps anything was possible.

"Everything's going to be alright," Dan said hopefully. He rolled onto his back and slid into a shallow gap, forcing the flashlight about, looking for the haphazard junctions of support that were protecting Kristin from the enormous weight overhead.

"But you're not trying to dig me out. Did she tell you not to?"

"How did you know that?" he asked, turning the flashlight ahead, examining the truncated pyramid of beams above her.

"I don't know."

"As long as she's around you'll know a lot of things without quite understanding why."

Kristin said nothing to this puzzling response. She studied Ellen's peaceful expression.

As Dan gripped and pulled gently at each beam and knee-brace, feeling for strength, Ellen spoke. "I don't think you can get to her from here. When ya touch things, when ya pull on 'em, I get a sense of their likely reaction. I don't think there's hardly a thing you could do on this fallen side without makin' it collapse."

Kristin watched her father ease out of the narrow space ahead.

"What are we going to do then?" he asked, standing and brushing off his hands.

"Let's work our way around the edges and feel our way along and see if we can find a path you can slide through, perhaps movin' a few things along the way, and get to her. Maybe then you could drag her out."

Dan heard voices. Sue was pleading, frustrated with the 911 dispatcher who was apparently asking detailed questions about location and circumstances.

Sue finally hung up and ran along the side of the barn searching for Dan. As she rounded the corner she caught sight of him laying on his back examining another spot. The harsh glare of the truck's headlights illuminated the scene. Kneeling beside him appeared to be the transparent, glasslike outline of a woman. The shape seemed to momentarily turn, fixing its eyes on Sue as she approached, and then simply disappeared. Sue squinted her eyes, puzzled.

Dan quickly scooted out.

"Wha ...?," Sue stammered, shaking her head. "Is there someone else here? I thought I saw a woman."

Dan quickly dismissed the notion. "Why don't you just go to the opening we first looked into and talk to Kristin until help arrives. I'm going to keep looking for a way to get to her." Not waiting for a response he turned and crouched back down along the rim of the barn.

Mere minutes passed before the distant sound of sirens echoed up the road. Soon they shattered the peaceful night air as the fire trucks and ambulance screamed up Main and along the banked curve approaching the farmhouse. Finally the private, courtyard like space between the line of trees and the farm buildings was crowded with emergency vehicles, their flashing lights slicing across the canopy of trees and the green, inverted barn roof.

Immediately, consultations began about the best way to get Kristin out. Firefighters with powerful flashlights were kneeling on the ground peering into every opening. The sound of engines, shouts of conversation, and the hissing crackle of police radios filled the air. Sue stepped back to give the men room. Dan came around the barn and dropped to the ground beside the apparent leader who pointed his light in at the trapped young woman.

Dan spoke up, breathless, "I've been here a little while examining the situation. I don't think you can get her out from this side."

The fireman turned to Dan and took in his comment without emotion before looking in again. "What makes ya' say that?"

"It just looks to me like if you pulled down any of this to get at her, it would trigger a collapse right over her head."

Dan scanned the crowd for a familiar, sympathetic face. Twenty years ago he knew nearly every man on the fire department. But these young men were all strangers, and each seemed to be examining him, questioning his qualifications to tell them how to do their job.

"I was the one who cut the space open to begin with," Dan put in quickly. "I had come-alongs tethered about the beams. I know how this thing goes together."

The commander, a big man with a barrel chest and neatly trimmed mustache, nodded insincerely. "Well, we'll all have a look and then discuss the best way to proceed."

For nearly twenty minutes Dan and four firemen moved about the shattered front of the barn in a tight group, discussing and debating moving in from various given points. Dan opposed each plan suggested by the other men. Twice, firefighters saw Dan stare blankly to the ground, apparently deep in thought, before pronouncing a spot unsafe.

One fireman whispered to another, "Guided by voices?" The firefighters became increasingly impatient with Dan's seemingly unfounded assertions of imminent danger.

The commander stopped them all beneath a tripod mounted trouble-light. Insects swirled about the glaring halogen light over his head. "Look," he said bluntly to Dan, "we'll use a saw to cut a couple openings in the back wall and see if there's any way in from there, but sooner or later we're gonna hafta do something and I'm," he pointed at himself with both hands in unison, "the one who's gonna make the call, not you," he pointed at Dan.

Dan searched the unsympathetic faces for support, then begrudgingly nodded in agreement.

Two holes were cut near the base of the weathered barn siding on the intact south face. One was impassable. But beyond the other was a small wedge-shaped pocket of open space big enough for a man to stand upright just within the opening. Overhead, the loft floor held fast against the south wall but fell to the ground ten feet ahead. There was a small gap where the floor met the ground, though big enough to crawl through, beyond it, Kristin could not be seen. Dan and the commander lay side by side in the dirt, examining the jumbled space with a flashlight. Above them, planks of flooring followed the fallen structure to the ground. Before them the shattered opening revealed another, wide, shallow passage, like a basement crawl space in an old house beneath the fallen roof, scattered and blocked with broken wood and debris.

The commander shook his head, saying simply, "Nope. It ain't gonna happen this way." They climbed back out of the opening in the siding where he pronounced, "We're going in from the front."

Dan ignored this for a moment, listening to the black sky. "No!" he barked. "That opening," he pointed urgently to the hole they had just crawled from. "That's the way to her."

"Look," the commander said, coming nearly nose to nose with Dan, "I know you mean well, I know it's your daughter in there, but I'm making the call," he thumbed back at his chest. He turned quickly as if Dan no longer existed, "Come on fellas, let's get back to the front and rip this motherfucker open."

With one hand Dan grabbed the commander's arm and jerked hard. "Don't do it. Just hear me out. You're gonna kill 'er."

"Restrain 'em," the commander ordered, pulling away and moving on.

A young police officer, half Dan's age, grabbed him by the arm. Dan tore away, scowling. "I ain't gonna freak out on nobody. I just think you're doing it the wrong way."

The commander turned back. "Fine then. You stand out there beside one of the trucks and out of our way."

As the group came around the front of the barn, Tom's Hummer bounded up the drive. He jumped out, still dressed in a button down collar and tie for the reunion. "What's happened?"

Sue went to him and explained.

"Aw hell," Tom shook his head to Sue. "Dan," he called down the length of a fire truck, "I know we've said some harsh things to each other these past couple days, but I want you to know I'll help in any way I can."

Dan nodded back vacantly.

The commander walked over and huddled close to Tom, whispering, "This guy a friend of yours?"

"Yeah," Tom said, loosening his necktie.

"Help us keep an eye on him, okay? I got a feeling he's might flip out or something. I just don't want him to get in the way."

"No problem," Tom nodded.

The commander returned to his men.

With a sledgehammer and a crowbar, the firemen began dismantling the lowest front lip of the barn. Dan frantically paced the ground before Sue and Tom and a fire truck. "They're doin' the wrong thing. It's gonna kill 'er."

Sue shook her head. "I don't know what's going on with you, but you need to step back, let go of your ego, and let the professionals do their thing."

"You don't understand," he said dismissively.

A fireman yanked the pull cord of a gas-powered circular saw. It screamed to life. He began slicing a line in the fallen barn roof. Blue, two-cycle smoke billowed and sparks spit into the protective mask he wore.

In an unexpected burst, Dan bolted past the firemen. "Stop him," the commander yelled. Tom reluctantly gave chase.

Dan, with Tom lumbering behind, raced frantically to the back of the barn and dove headfirst into the rough-cut opening. Tom struggled to follow, crawling slowly into the opening, catching his loosened necktie on a nail.

Dan heard the clatter behind him and desperately scurried ahead on all fours. He examined the space a moment, then dropped to his stomach and scooted into the small opening where the collapsed hayloft floor met the ground.

Maneuvering through the debris, propelled by his elbows like a soldier under barbed wire, he had almost disappeared when Tom grabbed his foot. Dan wrapped both arms around a shattered floor joist and tried to kick himself free.

Tom held fast. "Dan, for God's sake," he shouted, "come back out now. I know you're worried, but let the other fellas do their work. They don't need *two* people to rescue."

In a sudden flash, Ellen appeared, kneeling on the ground before Tom, her face just inches from his. Her teeth clenched, her voice thundered, "Let go of him!"

Startled, Tom let go, falling backward onto the ground. Dan snaked his way forward, out of reach.

Ellen glared at the fallen man, crawling toward him. Tom stared into her radiant, glowing face, trying to understand. She came nearer and his mind momentarily registered the receding layers of her being, that she was not human. This menacing, almost cartoon human shape moved toward him with an expression that said she meant to tear him to pieces. With his skin crawling, a wave of electricity passed across his scalp. The hair on the back of his neck stood up straight.

"Git out of here," she hissed.

Terrified, Tom scurried frantically backward on his heels and palms, struggling to get out the opening. Instead his back landed flat against the fieldstone foundation, knocking the wind out of him. He froze for a moment, gulping for air.

Ellen meant to scare him out of his skin and out of the barn for good. Kneeling over him, she reached out with one hand and clenched it around his throat. The tingling, icy grip forced a feminine scream from his mouth, nearly drowned out by the roaring drone of the circular saw still ripping through the shingles at the front of the fallen barn. Ellen sneered scornfully at him. He whimpered and struggled sideways to the opening, finally digging in his heels and kicking desperately at the ground, propelling himself clumsily out of the barn.

She peered out of the jagged opening at Tom lying in the grass. "You'll git worse if ya dig me up," she spat, taunting him.

Unaware that he was safe, Dan crawled onward on his stomach, wedging through small openings, over broken timbers, rotted hay, and splintered floorboards. By now powerful lights had been positioned at each broken opening along the north side, casting harsh, fractured shadows among the interior of the debris pile. Dan crawled to a dead end. He could go no farther and was still at least twenty feet from Kristin.

Outside, Tom ran toward the front of the barn with a pained expression of terror on his face, jerking his neck one way and then the other, looking fearfully over each shoulder, appearing to the others to be frantically running from something. A fireman grabbed his arm, "What happened?"

Tom's face was crimson, his nostrils flared and teeth tightly clenched as he clawed at his neck, as if trying desperately to tear free of something.

"It's cold. It's so cold," he whimpered, anxiously looking over his shoulder toward the back of the barn.

"What happened?" the fireman demanded.

Tom's expression sprang to awareness, as if just now realizing where he was. "U-um," he stammered, "he, he got away."

"He's in there?" the fireman pointed, arm outstretched at the barn, incredulous.

Tom nodded.

"Damn," the fireman grunted, pulling off his helmet and throwing it to the ground. He tapped the saw operator on the arm and motioned with an index finger across his neck to cut the engine. He turned to the commander. "That guy's in there."

The commander rolled his eyes. Hands on his hips, he stared at the ground, thinking. "Well, we need to go on and get her out and then hope he gets out the same way he got in." He dropped to his knees and ducked under the lip of the roof.

"Don't worry young lady," he called to Kristin. "We're done cuttin' for now. We're gonna use a crowbar and a sledge-hammer and open this up. Keep your face covered and we'll be there in a few minutes."

Deep in the debris pile, Dan closed his eyes and tried to catch his breath. He could feel Ellen near him. "What do I do now?" he asked, defeated.

"There are things you can move, things you can pull away to get at her, but ya have to act fast. They're 'bout to trigger a collapse. But ya have to be careful. Move the wrong thing and you'll trigger it yourself."

Exasperated, Dan demanded, "Okay, but what do I move right now to get beyond this point."

"It's gonna take forever fer me to point and explain. There's a faster way if yer willin'."

Dan looked down the length of his body to her kneeling at his feet. He knew what she meant. "Do it now. This is our chance. Do it before I have time to think about it."

Her eyes fixed intently on his. Glaring shards of light pierced the haphazard tunnel from the far outer edges where the firemen worked, illuminating thin clouds of dust that hung like fog in the air. Ellen's gently glowing form was sliced transparent in stripes by the beams of light. As if crawling forward to lie on top of Dan, she disappeared into him.

Once again, the adrenaline rush came to Dan, but more

intensely than ever before. The electric icy feel of Ellen's touch passed into deep warmth that ran like a powerful charge from his feet to his scalp. His form felt expanded under sudden pressure, as if overfilled with contents. His vision changed. He was seeing the world as he had during the vision of Jack in the family plot—the definitions of heat, the magnetic pull of gravity, the fear and anticipation radiating off his own arms, the ability to choose a perspective and see it. It was seeing like thinking. In the same way anyone could shuffle through memories and ideas, he could shuffle through ways of seeing, concentrating on heat, or focusing only on light. It was peaceful and fascinating.

"Focus! Hurry!" she urged him.

The force of gravity bled color on the objects around him. Dan could see a harmless jumble of splintered wood before him. The thin, shimmering rainbow ribbons of color were intense on those bearing great weight, and barely noticeable on those that didn't. He twisted around in the space and kicked at a line of boards with his heals, knocking them clear. He spun back around and crawled over them, tearing open his forearm on a nail. The pain came more like an idea than real pain. He moved on.

From within the debris pile, the truck engines and the generators powering the work lights drowned out the specifics of instructions the firemen yelled back and forth. Still, the dull thud of a sledgehammer striking a timber broke the air and Dan could sense the vibrations reverberate through the accidental structure around him. "Kristin!" he yelled. She raised her head and turned to the right, but could see nothing. Then she caught a glimpse of him moving through a beam of light. "D-a-d-d-y!" she called out.

"Hang on," he yelled.

She was ten feet away. A timber cut across his path touching the ground at one end. Again he spun around and kicked at the beam, breaking it free from the splintered knee-brace that held it in place. It fell to the ground. Dan hurriedly scrambled past it and crawled right up to her. He reached through the beams, floor joists, and rusted bailing wire that trapped her and ran his hand through her hair. He was trembling wildly and where his fingers touched her neck she again shuddered at the faint icy shock she'd felt when touched by Ellen. She turned to him and began crying softly. The shimmering depth behind his eyes scared her.

There was a fireman several feet in from the lip of the fallen roof. He repositioned his work light and caught a glimpse of Dan. He yelled above the hoarse hum of the generators, "Just hold on there and we'll have you both out in a minute."

"No!" Dan yelled, defiantly. "Don't come any farther. Don't move anything else. If you pull out those beams that whole thing is gonna come down on all three of us!"

The fireman shook his head in exasperation. He called back over his shoulder to the men behind him, "Throw me the chain."

Dan surmised what was about to happen. They were going to put a log chain around the most crucial beams and pull them out with a come-along. He frantically started pulling at a hand-hewn floor joist wedged to the ground and running along Kristin's body. He used a broken piece of floorboard to gouge at the dirt holding it in place.

From Kristin's other side, the fireman worked to lace the chain around the mortise and tenon joint of two, eight-by-eight beams. "You know your Dad loves you and wants to save you, but he's let his emotions cloud his thinking," he yelled to her while he worked. "If I don't move these beams, he'll have to drag you out the long way, underneath this whole mess. But once I get this out, you can just slide right out this way." He smiled warmly at her and slid back out the front, dragging the end of the chain with him.

"Don't listen to him," Dan barked. "When he moves that, this whole thing's gonna come down on us."

Kristin struggled to turn toward her father. "How do you know, Daddy?" she asked calmly.

"She told me," he said, "the spirit that came to you and watched over you. She knows these things. She sees things they can't see."

His voice was different. It didn't sound right to Kristin. And there was a foreign look in his eye. "Daddy, I'm frightened."

"Of them or me?" Dan asked, splitting glances between her searching face and the ground where he dug.

"Who is she Daddy?"

"She's a spirit trapped here. She lived here and raised her children on this land."

"What does she want with you? What does she want with us?"

Dan's digging was interrupted by a stubborn panel of wire fence nailed to the joist. "She's lonely," he said. "You would be, too."

"Maybe she's sending us in the wrong direction so we'll get killed and she won't be alone anymore."

Dan shook his head, "You been watching too many movies."

His digging exposed the bottom edge of the joist but it was still bound by rusted wire. He tossed the stick aside. "I've always taken care of you—I've always protected you. You have to trust me Sugarcube."

He jerked desperately at the fence wire. It was the last thing holding the joist in place. A sharp, rusted wire end came free, ripping a gash in the palm of his hand. Ignoring the wound, he frantically pulled at the remaining rusty strands of wire, but they held fast. Dan could hear a log chain clanging up ahead and knew he had little time. He let out a frustrated whimper, looking around him for another option. With a start, it dawned on him he had a tool.

With his bloody palm he fumbled at his hip, pulling the all-in-one tool from his belt. He struggled to wedge the crotch of the plier jaws against the fence wire, cutting one strand and then another, finally untangling the mass. He grabbed the freed floor joist and pulled it away, exposing the length of Kristin's body.

He leaned over her and lovingly caressed her forehead. "You know what she wants more than anything else? I didn't know it until now, but more than anything else she wants to have some meaningful effect on this world. That's what she misses. That's what she's doing now."

Dan gripped her under one arm. "We don't have much time. Try to slide out."

Kristin gingerly maneuvered out on her back, using her elbows and heels. She cried out as it sent a shot of pain through her chest.

"Stop," Dan said. "Let me pull you out."

"Okay," she whimpered.

"Lean up on your elbows," Dan offered quickly.

He scooted around behind her and slipped his legs under her arms. Sitting, he gripped her under each arm, her hips cradled between his legs. Kristin gritted her teeth in pain. Dan heard a truck being positioned in front of the barn and the chain rattling. They were preparing to hitch it to the truck.

"Hang on," Dan barked, "we really gotta move fast."

He scooted backward on his bottom, pushing with his heels. Where headroom allowed, he crouched on his knees and crawled backward, dragging Kristin over boards and across debris.

"She's buried there in that graveyard, isn't she?" Kristin groaned over her shoulder, breathless with pain. "That's why you cried when Tom said he was digging it up?"

"Yes," Dan grunted, pulling her over a fallen beam.

"Why isn't she in heaven?" Kristin asked.

Without hesitation Dan replied, "Trying to hang onto things that can't be held—trying to change things that can't be changed."

They were nearing the small opening to the cavity at the back of the barn.

The chain rattled beyond them, toward the front of the barn. The truck engine revved. Dan let go of Kristin.

"I'm gonna crawl through this hole and then pull you through, he said simply. As he wedged through the opening, a voice shouted at the front of the barn, "Go ahead."

The chain rattled and the engine revved again. A sharp clank told Dan the chain's slack was gone and the end was near. He hurried through the hole. Timbers began to groan throughout the structure. Kristin struggled on her elbows and heels, trying to follow on her own power. The pain of this backward journey was sending her body into shock, but she willed herself ahead. Her face was pale. Her expression was impassive. She was moving unconsciously, propelled by adrenaline and instinct.

Dan called, "Lay back and throw out your hands." She did so without question. From the other side Dan reached through the opening, grabbed Kristin's outstretched hands and pulled her recklessly through the narrow, jagged hole. She screamed in agony.

The truck pulled forward. The chain yanked at the beams that had once protected Kristin. The haphazard structure overhead began to clatter and shake.

The fire truck edged forward. The long beams that had acted as a kick-stand for the south wall were pulled out of place and collapsed the roof completely at the point where Kristin had been trapped, with a sharp, emphatic crash. The commander yelled, "STOP!" but was nearly drowned out by Sue's piercing scream.

It was too late. The standing south wall began to quiver on its foundation. In the wedge-shaped cavity where Dan and Kristin had finally landed, the sill plate twisted atop the foundation. A fieldstone broke free of the mortar, tumbling to the ground.

Sue, Tom, and the firemen watched breathless and heartsick as the south wall teetered and convulsed while bits of the nearer, half-fallen section sank lower.

Dan could feel the wall roll like a vertical wave straight overhead and could see it rack against the foundation like the tail of a whip. Dirt and powdered wood-rot filtered down from overhead like snowfall in hell. He kept moving backward, pulling Kristin across the dirt floor, on toward the saw-cut opening.

Overhead the inverted roof tore free of the eaves of the south wall and crumbled downward. The standing wall shuddered and flexed wildly, ready to follow the roof. Finally it did, tipping toward the debris pile. The wall's mid-point hit the fallen roof and slowly ripped free of the foundation. As Dan scooted backward through the saw cut opening, dragging his daughter behind him, the wall sections on either side lifted off the foundation and passed him moving in the opposite direction. Dan and Kristin tumbled into the grass. The intact wall tipped like a teeter-totter against the debris pile before snapping in the center and joining the heap.

Out front, Sue searched the hopeless outcome in disbelief, looking for a reason to believe anything other than what seemed obvious. She turned to Tom, gripped his shirt at the shoulder, and pleaded, "You saw him in there, right? Dan was in there going after Kristin?"

Tom nodded vacantly.

"Maybe he saved her," Sue sputtered, "maybe they're out." She searched Tom's face as he took in the wrecked barn. Finally she broke into sobs.

The commander cast a heavy sidelong glance at Tom holding Sue as she cried into his shoulder. He turned to a policeman. "You better call forensics."

In the tall grass behind the barn, Dan and Kristin lay side by side, breathing heavily. Dan's once-white shirt was torn and blackened, bloody on the arm and palm where he'd been cut. Kristin's blonde hair was dark with dirt and tangled with bits of hay and splinters of wood. Dan lay on his back staring blankly up at the sky. Kristin lay on her stomach, her cheek to the grass, watching her father catch his breath. He gasped for air, his chest rising and falling convulsively. There was a shimmering glow to the edges of his form, like mist caught in light.

Then, as if steam rising off his body, Ellen's form lifted out of him, taking the glow from Dan's shape with her. Stretched out straight above him, she hovered just an inch or two clear of his chest, staring straight upward, her arms crossed on her chest. Ellen turned her head, meeting Kristin's eyes. She smiled, satisfied and reassuringly, then disappeared.

From around the barn came the thundering of feet and the yells of rescue workers. Exhausted, Kristin fell once more into blackness.

CHAPTER 15

Dan sat with Sue at the hospital long after it seemed necessary, long after his cuts were stitched and Kristin was pronounced safe and stable. She had two broken ribs, a concussion, and a lot of scrapes and bruises. She was asleep. They'd keep her overnight.

Dan agreed that Kristin would be more comfortable at Sue's house. He told Sue he would gather up her things and move them to the 16th Street house the next day. Dan stood to leave. They passed a few awkward moments while the waiting room TV droned late night infomercials.

"You're a marvelous man, Dan," Sue whispered. "She'd be dead now if it weren't for you. What you did was a miracle. Whatever possessed you?"

"I guess we don't know what we're capable of until the circumstances present themselves."

She stared at him, taking in his comment and thinking forward to something else connected. "Will you take the job in Warsaw?"

"Yes," Dan said simply. "As you said in the car earlier tonight, this is our chance. It's not a happy ending, but maybe it's the only real way to salvage something of our ... oh I don't know ... self-respect ... happiness?"

Sue nodded slowly, knowing he was right. "And you'll be gone from this town," she said.

"Yep."

"You'll do a fine job. We both know that."

He bent and gave Sue a kiss on the forehead. "Bye now," he said, then walked through the lobby and out the automatic doors. He stood along the edge of the emergency lane roundabout. Forcing his hands into his pockets he gazed up at the black sky and thought of Ellen.

He felt as awake as he'd ever felt. There'd be no sleeping anytime soon. He asked the hospital taxi to drive him home and directed the driver to the Ballard farm. The elderly volunteer squinted hard at Dan as he stepped out of the van in the middle of the night along the dark, curved stretch of Main. He called, "Now wait a minute," but Dan disappeared into the black, up the drive of the old deserted farmhouse.

He made his way along the shattered pile that had been the barn, only to find Ellen standing there beyond the line of trees as he had so often found her before. Purposefully, she didn't watch him approach, but he examined her closely, looking at her layers, the soft glowing outer shimmer, the textured weave beneath what appeared to be real skin and real cloth. And even that sparkled, too, just enough to suggest something else lay beneath. She even turned away as he drew closer, as if protecting herself from examination.

"What's the point?" he muttered. "I've seen everything there is to see about you ... and you've seen all there is to see of me." He reached out to touch her shoulder and felt his hand fall within the electric ice of the intense, though contradictory, waves that made up her being.

"I know what you've seen," she said, "I just don't know what it looks like ... to you, I mean."

Dan took in the glowing landscaping lights of the first occupied house of the subdivision far to the south.

She turned abruptly to him. "A hundred and thirty-five years ago my husband married another woman and they made over the house into another style. Another twenty-five years later the horses began to disappear. Add to that a thousand other little changes ... changes from the way I knew things at my best. Yet, the way I knew things at my best were imprinted on me ... on my soul," she pressed her hand against her chest.

"We accept some sense of how things are, what the shapes of things are around us, and we expect that it will always be that way. We may gain a few pounds—a few gray hairs—but our personal vision of ourselves stays the same. Do ya see what I mean?"

Dan ran a hand through his salt and pepper hair. "Oh yeah."

"All these years," she went on, "I've been seein' things as I chose to see 'em. I knew it wasn't real, wasn't a real reflection of what was goin' on around me, but still I allowed my love of this place and the part I once played in it to freeze me in a hollow sort of limbo between the real and the imagined."

She turned to him, searching his eyes for the under-standing she knew was there. "You can only do that for so long. You can only demoralize yourself to a certain point, away from that moment when you were at your best, beyond which you become a slave to fantasy. At some point ... when things change so much ... you have to accept that your ... imprinted view," she pressed hard against her chest again, "can't stall the inevitable. You have to find a place to matter. It can't happen secondhand through another person. It has to be you actin' upon the world.

"There's a place for me now and it's not here. It used to be here ... but not anymore."

She gave him space to understand, to respond, but he didn't. "D-Don't you see," she stammered, "you're fascinated with what I am, and I'm fascinated with what you are. But as much as we may admire one another, neither of us are what we should be.

"Maybe ... sometimes ... havin' things forced on you is the only way to make you move."

It was still dark out when Dan made the banked curve of north Main. The sun would be up soon. Almost without him noticing, summer had waned. He pulled into the driveway and got out.

The last of it would be all gone tomorrow. Two huge maple trees that didn't follow the landscaping plan lay on their sides between the house and the carriage shed. The house was stripped. The barn, milk house, grain bin, and carriage shed were now a single useless pile, the shattered wood and brick mixed with dirt, pushed to one side to move them out of the way. A huge, two-acre-sized gouge, fifteen feet deep, had been dug in the ground where the barn had set, soon to be the retention pond. The gravestones were gone from the family plot. A yellow backhoe sat in the middle, piles of dirt all around.

"I'm goin' with ya," Ellen's voice spoke gently from behind him.

Dan turned, hands in his pockets. He watched her examining the boxes and furniture stacked in the back of the truck and bound tight with bungee cords.

"It was really a beautiful place," she said, turning to scan her ruined landscape, being remade anew.

"Things change," Dan said.

Ellen smiled sadly and closed her eyes, nodding her head. "Yes, things change."

"It was beautiful in the wrong way for today," Dan sighed. "It was beautiful in a way that feeds your soul, but to be saved, it needed to be beautiful in a way that feeds your wallet."

She came close, narrowing an eye at him and whispered urgently, "You'll do this for me, won't you? You'll take me with you? We'll leave together."

Dan examined her gentle face. He knew what she meant. With a lump in his throat, he nodded his head.

Ellen had never approached the truck before, never purposefully stood so close with the engine running. It wasn't nearly as intimidating as a team of muscular horses, straining as they pulled a heavy load, but still it was foreign ... and intimidating.

Dan opened the door for her.

She positioned herself inside awkwardly, taking an upright posture, as if sitting on a bench instead of reclining as modern folks would do in a car. Dan closed the door and came around and sat behind the wheel. He put his hand on the gearshift and hesitated. "Are you sure you want to do this?" he asked her.

She cast a hesitant sidelong glance at him, her shimmering layers illuminated in the gentle, green dashboard lights,

"Don't give me time to think, just go," she half whispered, "It's my chance, now, with you by my side. I can't let it slip by. Just go, Dan."

He pulled back on the stick and they moved forward slowly. As they made the soft curve of the driveway and met the road, Ellen looked over her shoulder, through the back window at the pile of lumber that had once been the barn and at the stripped house, windows and doors and front porch bare and empty, the downed trees and bulldozed cemetery. It all looked naked and dirty, unkempt and unloved ... doomed. She forced her eyes back toward the road as Dan pulled onto the asphalt and turned right, heading east.

He tried to force his gaze ahead; to avoid whatever was about to happen. But as the covered bridge came into view he turned and watched Ellen close her eyes, lay back in the seat, and cross her arms on her chest.

Beyond the line of trees where they sat and talked often, where the ravine gave way to the south of the road, her body, her form, started to pull apart, scattering at the edges like a pile of damp leaves in a strong wind. Luminescent pieces of the layers of her soul and spirit and the light waves echoing the shape of her former self pulled loose bit by bit and swirled about the center of her form, bits blowing out the open window and through the glass of the windshield.

Dan jabbed at the tears running down his face with the palm of his hand, then stretched his arm out, trying to feel the center of her, her form just barely remaining. An intense lightness passed through his hand, the sensation of it having fallen asleep. And then in a sudden burst, what remained of her shape fell in upon itself and scattered out the open window and up into the air, like embers drawn up a chimney.

She was gone.

ACKNOWLEDGEMENTS

Many thanks to those who touched this manuscript along the way; Joe Formichella, Dan Logan, Linda Clarkbaker, Suzanne Clar Purewal, Jack Meyer, Kerry Brooks, and Lynn Hopper. Thanks as well to Shari Smith, Susan Crandall, Bill Kenley, and Ted and Mary Sue Rowland who supported and encouraged my writing.

ABOUT THE AUTHOR

Kurt Meyer's writing, whether as newspaper columnist, novelist or blogger, chronicles and explores the changing cultural landscape of Midwestern small town life. He's worked as a realtor specializing in marketing historic properties, has restored multiple Victorian-era homes and co-founded the annual literary journal, *Polk Street Review.*

You can keep up with Kurt at www.kurtameyer.com.

3 1690 01895 7770

19-1

CARMEL CLAY PUBLIC LIBRARY
Renewal Line: (317) 814-3936
www.carmel.lib.in.us

WITHDRAWN FROM
CARMEL CLAY
PUBLIC LIBRARY

CPSIA information can be obtained at www.ICGtesting.com
Printed in the USA
LVOW11s1800090216

474361LV00007B/831/P